Reaching into the back

from her bag and tapped

moment, the car rocked as

passenger side of the car with a loud thud. She jumped, dropping the phone in surprise when the door was flung open and someone threw himself onto the passenger seat. Momentarily startled, she stared at the man before finding her voice. “Hey, what do you think you’re doing?”

The stranger ignored her and turned to look over his shoulder. He pulled the car door shut as he shoved a duffel bag into the back seat. “Drive.”

“What? No, get out of my car.” The cheek of the man; this clearly wasn’t simply someone who had got into the car thinking she was someone else.

He turned on her with an explicit curse. “I said drive!”

Surprise and disbelief turned to fear, and Willow fumbled to unclip her seatbelt. Strong fingers curled around her upper arm, preventing her from moving as she reached for the door lever.

In the dim light, she saw the gun pointing at her stomach and drew in a strangled breath, barely able to believe what she was seeing. The wing mirror on the passenger door suddenly shattered in an explosion of glass shards, and the stranger ducked in surprise, releasing his grip on her arm.

He swore, shifting once again to look over his shoulder, his eyes gleaming in the lamplight as he turned his head. “For God’s sake, drive!”

Praise for Ellie Gray

Her debut novel, Beauty and the Recluse, won First Place in the East Texas Writers Guild Book Awards 2016.

Her novel, Warwick's Mermaid, won a Chill with a Book Premier Reader's Award in 2018.

Winter Storm

by

Ellie Gray

This is a work of fiction. Names, characters, places, and incidents are either the product of the author's imagination or are used fictitiously, and any resemblance to actual persons living or dead, business establishments, events, or locales, is entirely coincidental.

Winter Storm

Contact Information: info@thewildrosepress.com

Cover Art by *Debbie Taylor*

The Wild Rose Press, Inc.
PO Box 708
Adams Basin, NY 14410-0708
Visit us at www.thewildrosepress.com

Publishing History
First Edition, 2021
Trade Paperback ISBN 978-1-5092-3633-6
Digital ISBN 978-1-5092-3634-3

Published in the United States of America

Dedication

For Mum and Dad.
I miss you.
xxx

Chapter One

When the traffic light turned red, Willow Daniels pulled the car to a halt on the lonely side street and gripped the steering wheel hard. Briefly closing her eyes in frustration, she silently cursed herself at being utterly lost.

A simple wrong turn after leaving the train station led to mounting confusion as she endeavoured to navigate her way through the streets of York city center in the dark. Getting into the wrong lane, then reading street signs too late led to further, and now obvious, wrong turns. She found herself well outside the center, and in the middle of what appeared to be an industrial estate.

Deserted at this late hour of the evening, the streets were empty, with no one around to ask for directions. And now the occasional, drifting wisps of snow had evolved into a steady fall of large flakes, swirling, and glistening in the soft glow of the streetlights.

Willow blew out a long breath; everything was fine, she just needed to pull over somewhere, get out her phone and use the satnav function to find her way home.

As the light turned green, she eased the car forward, aware of the thickening layer of snow covering the tarmac, and not wanting the car to skid on the slippery surface.

"Could have turned in there…and there," she muttered, as she saw the potential pull in opportunities too late. "Oh, for heaven's sake, Willow, just turn in somewhere!"

Shaking her head at her indecision, she saw what looked like a carpark at the front of a large warehouse, and flicked the indicator switch on before pulling in through the gap in the low wall surrounding the building. She left the engine idling and sat back in her seat, flexing her shoulders to ease her tension as she stared through the windscreen. The festive tunes on the radio, and the snowflakes drifting down unhurriedly from the sky soothed her frustration.

It was an industrial scene, with low, squat functional buildings lining the road, and taller but equally non-descript warehouses stretching out behind them. But the harsh, straight lines of the buildings were softened by the dim light, and Willow imagined an artist might capture this scene with a moody, slightly out of focus composition of grays and yellows, brush strokes recreating the shadows on the walls and lending an element of interest to the otherwise dull concrete.

A frown creased her forehead. If this snow continued or got any heavier, there was a risk she might not make it back. Reaching into the back seat, Willow took the phone from her bag and tapped in her password.

The next moment, the car rocked as something slammed into the passenger side of the car with a loud thud. She jumped, dropping the phone in surprise when the door was flung open and someone threw himself onto the passenger seat. Momentarily startled, she stared at the man before finally finding her voice. "Hey, what do you think you're doing?"

The stranger ignored her and turned to look over his shoulder. He pulled the car door shut as he shoved a duffel bag into the back seat. "Drive."

"What? No, get out of my car." The cheek of the man; this clearly wasn't simply someone who had got into the car thinking she was someone else.

He turned on her with an explicit curse. "I said drive!"

Surprise and disbelief turned to fear, and Willow fumbled to unclip her seatbelt. Strong fingers curled around her upper arm, preventing from moving as she reached for the door lever.

In the dim light, she saw the gun pointing at her stomach and drew in a strangled breath, barely able to believe what she was seeing. The wing mirror on the passenger door suddenly shattered in an explosion of glass shards. The stranger ducked, releasing his grip on her arm.

He swore, shifting once again to look over his shoulder, his eyes gleaming in the lamplight as he turned his head. "For God's sake, drive!"

The urgency in his voice transferred itself to her. Putting the car into gear, she slammed her foot down hard on the accelerator and gasped as the car leapt forward, slithering in the snow as the tyres fought for traction. Battling to keep the car under control, she pulled out onto the road without checking for traffic, grateful the roads were almost deserted.

The stranger was still looking over his shoulder, breathing hard, his gun still pointing at her. As the traffic light turned amber, and she automatically slowed the car, he turned back.

"Keep going." He pushed the gun a little closer after she shook her head. "I mean it."

She gave a small moan, hunching her shoulders and squinting her eyes as she braced for possible impact. The car shot through the lights just as they turned red.

"Left here," he threw over his shoulder, his attention still behind them. He ground out further directions, seemingly at random, but eventually blew out a long breath, and turned to face forward.

As he sank back into the seat, he hissed as if in pain, but didn't speak. Risking a glance at his profile as they passed under the glow of a streetlamp, she had the impression of a lean face and a straight nose.

"Keep your eyes on the road." His voice was soft, his gaze focused on the area ahead.

"What happened to the wing mirror?" Knuckles white, Willow's fingers ached from gripping the steering wheel. She flexed them, wincing at the pain. She bit her lip when she saw how much her hands were shaking. Her legs were shaking too, so hard her foot threatened to slip off the accelerator pedal. She cast a fearful glance toward the gun. It was still pointing toward her. "Did someone shoot it?"

When he didn't answer, she tried again. "Where am I am driving to?"

For a moment she thought he was going to continue ignoring her, but then he leaned forward to switch off the radio with a snap of his fingers. He massaged his forehead as if he had a headache and closed his eyes. "Just drive."

They drove in silence for a while, until she realized they had somehow made their way back into the city center. Street signs directed her back to familiar roads.

She drove instinctively, without thinking. There were one or two other cars on the roads now. Dare she risk trying to pull over and escape? Although she knew there was good reason to be frightened, she sensed she was in no danger, despite the stranger holding her at gunpoint.

His voice was soft, gentle even, and he held the gun toward her as if he'd forgotten about it. Even as she thought this, he relaxed his hand, resting the gun on his knees. He shifted his position, groaning a little.

From the corner of her eye she saw him pull his right hand from beneath his jacket and blow out a breath. "I need your scarf."

"What?" Willow risked a quick glance at him before turning her concentration back to the road.

"Your scarf." He reached across to gently pull the length of cloth from around her neck.

Once more taking her eyes from the road, she looked down at his hand. It was stained with what appeared to be a lot of dark liquid. Looking back at the road, she quickly corrected the car's direction as she tried to make sense of what she had just seen. He folded up the scarf and placed it carefully under his jacket, hissing in pain. Her heart missed a beat in sudden comprehension.

"Oh my God, is that blood? Are you hurt?" She automatically eased her foot off the accelerator pedal as he twisted his head to look at her. "Do we need to get you to a hospital? To the police?"

"If you don't keep driving—" he snapped, then clamped his mouth shut. He took a deep breath in through his nose. When he spoke again, his voice was quiet and calm, but brooked no argument. "No police, no hospitals. Just drive."

Her stomach churned as she concentrated on driving through the snow. The city was well behind them, and she drove deeper into the countryside, but that wasn't the reason for her unease. She couldn't stop thinking about the blood staining his hand. It had been a lot of blood.

His quiet voice broke into her troubled thoughts, making her jump. "Believe it or not, I'm one of the good guys."

His eyes remained closed, his hand still beneath the jacket, pressing her scarf against whatever injury he had sustained. He made no further comment, and after a while, his breathing grew shallow. Willow bit her lip. Had he lost consciousness or fallen asleep? Should she try and wake him? In the end, she left him to sleep; it was taking all her concentration to drive through the increasingly heavy snowfall.

Nearly an hour later, she pulled up outside her garage in the narrow ten-foot behind her small terraced house, deep in the heart of rural North Yorkshire. It was well past midnight. She sank back into her seat, squeezing her eyes shut and drawing in deep breaths of relief. She'd made it.

A quick glance at her passenger confirmed he was still asleep or unconscious. The sight of his pale face reminded her of the blood she'd seen staining his hand and stirred her into action.

The ground crunched beneath her feet, and she gasped as her foot sunk into the thick snow, instantly soaking her tights. A cold shiver rippled through her body. She pushed open the gate in the low fence enclosing her back garden and hurried down the path. For one heart-stopping moment, she slipped in the snow, arms wheeling in the air, before righting herself and grasping the door handle.

She unlocked her door, kicked off her shoes, and ran through the kitchen and up the stairs to the spare bedroom. She switched on the light. Blinking in the sudden brightness, she darted to the bed and pulled back the duvet. Next, she grasped the blanket from the chair by the window and spread it over the bedsheet. With a nod of satisfaction, she ran back downstairs. Slipping her feet back into her sodden shoes, she ran out to the car, opened the passenger door, and crouched by the stranger's side.

Even in the moonlight she could see the gray cast to his face.

"Hey, wake up." When he didn't stir, she touched his shoulder, gently shaking him. He remained unresponsive. "Please. You need to wake up."

In a flash, his fingers closed painfully around her forearm. He pulled her half into the car against him, the gun in his other hand pressing hard underneath her chin and forcing her head up. She struggled to breathe.

"I'm sorry, I'm sorry. Please don't. It's okay," Willow held her hands up, palms open in a conciliatory gesture. She closed her eyes, terrified he was going to shoot her. The door frame pressed painfully into her thigh as she lay awkwardly in his grip, half in—half out of the car. "It's okay."

He relaxed his hold on her arm, and relief flooded through her when she opened her eyes to see his gaze sharpen, then blink in obvious confusion.

Willow sank onto the cold snow. It instantly

soaked through her skirt as she clasped her hands together to prevent them from shaking. Her heart was pounding so hard in her chest, she thought it might actually fracture her ribs. The stranger groaned behind her, and she turned to see him adjusting the scarf against his side.

"I need to get you into the house. Can you walk?"

Though he looked dazed and disoriented, he didn't resist when she gently pulled him from the car. She slung his right arm over her shoulder and gripped his waist, taking his weight when his knees buckled beneath him. His left hand, still clutching the gun, was clamped against his side, and he groaned when she urged him down the path.

She wasn't sure just how she managed to get him up the stairs, but they made it somehow. She helped him onto the bed, easing him back onto the blanket. Now what? After a moment's hesitation, she ran down to the kitchen and shut the back door on the freezing night. The house was cold, and she gritted her teeth to stop them from chattering. Turning on the heating, she gathered her first aid kit, a bowl of hot water and clean towels.

Hesitating at the foot of the bed, she stared down at the stranger. He hadn't moved, and his eyes remained closed. His leather jacket had fallen open to reveal her blood-soaked scarf loosely resting against his hip. She needed to know if the wound was as bad as the amount of blood suggested it might be. Moving to the side of the bed, she gingerly lifted the hem of his black T-shirt.

"Oh my God!" Snatching back her hand, she turned away from the sight of the long, gaping wound in his side and the blood flowing steadily onto the blanket.

Pressing the back of her hand against her lips, fighting against nausea, she shook her head. She could not do this. This man was seriously injured, and she had no idea what to do. She wasn't a nurse, wasn't used to dealing with things like this. Lifting her gaze, she caught sight of her reflection in the bedroom window, pale and wide-eyed, and closed her eyes.

Come on, Willow. No one else can help him. He's going to bleed to death unless you do something.

Squaring her shoulders, she turned back to the bed. Stemming the flow of blood from the awful wound had to be her priority. Was it safe to move him? What if she made it worse? She hesitated, but the nauseating, coppery scent of blood forced her into action. Doing nothing wasn't an option.

Leaning over him, she was struck with the sudden memory of his instinctive reaction when she had moved him earlier, of his strength when he pulled her into the car, despite his wound, and of the gun being thrust under her chin. Heart thumping painfully in her chest, she reached out a trembling hand to ease the gun from his fingers, tensing herself for any sign he might instinctively react as he had done before. But he didn't move, and she placed the gun on the bedside cabinet.

Deliberately averting her gaze from his wound, she carefully pressed her blood-soaked scarf against his side beneath his t-shirt, before slipping her hands underneath his arms and pulling him toward her. Lord, he was heavy, almost a dead weight. She closed her eyes briefly. *Don't even think it.*

As she pulled him up into a sitting position, she leaned herself back until she was sitting on the side of the bed. The cold, wet skirt brought a grimace of distaste and discomfort as she took the stranger's weight, his head resting on her shoulder. He made no effort to either assist or pull against her, but he groaned at the movement. She breathed a small sigh of relief at this sign of life.

With some difficulty, she managed to remove the jacket, dropping it on the floor, before easing his arms from his T-shirt, favouring his right side, and pulling it over his head. Trying not to disturb the scarf still covering his side, she gently laid him back down.

After taking a moment to catch her breath, she walked around to the opposite side of the bed. Grasping his left shoulder and hip, she pulled him onto his side toward her. He groaned again, his fingers twitching reflexively, but didn't open his eyes. She whispered a hurried sorry but didn't relent. With one hand on his shoulder, she grabbed a pillow and quickly placed it behind his hip to prevent him from rolling onto his back. She pulled his left arm forward to rest on the bed to counterbalance his weight and leave his wounded side exposed.

She eyed the scarf, breathing out a long breath as she plucked up the courage to do what she had to do next. Rivulets of blood ran from beneath the scarf, across his stomach and onto the blanket. She needed to act quickly.

Without further thought, she grasped the scarf and dropped it onto the wooden floorboards next to his jacket. A brief, incongruous thought flashed through her mind that it was lucky she didn't have a pale carpet here in the spare bedroom. That thought quickly fled as she stared down at him. The whole of his left side was awash with blood. The sight of the wide, gaping wound resulted in another wave of nausea rising to the back of her throat.

"Come on, Willow." She picked up a towel and dipped it in the bowl of hot water. "You've got this. Don't think about it."

Wringing out the towel, she gently wiped the blood from his side. If anything, it looked even worse now that she could see the injury clearly. She quickly pressed the towel against his torso, closing her eyes as she forced herself to think. The only way to stop the bleeding was to close the wound. But it was so deep, the edges of the wound so wide, it clearly needed more than a simple dressing.

She rummaged in the first aid box, one hand still pressing the towel against his wound, frowning when she saw the packet of butterfly strips. Shaking the packet open, she eyed the thin, white strips. They would have to do.

After gingerly lifting the towel, blood immediately pooled in the wound. She quickly clamped the towel back in place as a wave of dizziness washed over her.

Okay, okay. You need to do this. Don't think of him as a man, as a human, just think of this as a problem. You need to bring both sides of the wound together and hold them there. Simple.

Willow lifted the towel once more and, after a brief glance at his face, resolutely focussed on the wound. Spreading her fingers wide to reach either side of the wound, she brought her middle finger and thumb carefully toward each other, pulling both sides of the wound together. Studiously ignoring the blood running down his stomach, she winced when he groaned and flinched. With her other hand, she eased one of the strips from the packet.

Breathing long, deep breaths through her nose, she used the strip to secure the edges of his skin together. Working quickly, she applied more strips until the wound was closed at last, and the bleeding stopped. Finally, she placed a longer strip vertically across each row of strips, as suggested in the instructions on the packet. She eyed her handiwork critically. She wasn't convinced they would hold such a deep laceration, but it would just have to do.

After wiping away the remaining traces of blood from his skin, she applied a clean, dry dressing before attending to another, smaller cut she had noticed on his shoulder blade.

It was done, over. She removed the pillow from behind his hip, and gently eased him onto his back. Breathing a shaky sigh of relief, she turned to sit on the edge of the bed, head dropping to her chest, and closed her eyes.

When she opened them again, her gaze fell on her hands, covered in the stranger's blood. She looked away in distaste, but it seemed there was blood everywhere: her hands, the towels, her scarf, his T-shirt. Her stomach squirmed as she took a breath; she could even taste it in the back of her throat.

Her chest tightened in sudden panic. Leaping to her feet, she gathered up all the blood-soaked clothing and towels, and ran downstairs. She piled everything into the washing machine, along with detergent and a good dose of stain remover and snapped it onto a wash cycle.

She then fled to the bathroom and turned on the taps, feverishly soaping and rinsing her hands under the flowing water until it ran clear. Leaning over the basin, she rested her forehead against the cool mirror, taking in long, deep breaths.

After a little while, she felt able to return to the spare bedroom where the stranger remained unconscious on the bed. Someone had clearly tried to kill this man, tried to take his life. It was something she just didn't comprehend. Who would do such a thing? Why would they do such a thing?

Just for a moment, she thought he wasn't breathing, and her heart missed a beat. After a few tense seconds, his chest rose slightly, and she heaved a sigh of relief. He was alive.

With his wound now dressed, she looked at him as he lay, bare-chested on the bed. Slender, with a taught, athletically muscled physique, his features were finely chiselled, with a straight nose and defined cheekbones. His lips, although pale and bloodless, were slim and well-shaped.

Her gaze fell upon the gun, where she had left it on the bedside table. *What on earth should she do with that?* She had brought this stranger into her house, but it would be particularly foolish to leave the weapon within easy reach.

With a grimace of distaste, she picked up the gun and, holding it gingerly between her finger and thumb, took it to her own room. Looking around, she considered her options. After a moment, she pulled out a box from underneath her bed, filled with various handmade Christmas decorations, and buried the gun at the bottom.

She looked at her bed, and a wave of weariness washed over her, wanting nothing more than to climb under the duvet and drift into a dreamless sleep.

Deliberately turning away, she returned to the spare room, stopping for a moment in the doorway to take in the odd scene. A half- clothed man who had recently held her at gunpoint, now lay in her bed. Despite her weariness, despite the gun he had held under her chin, she had no regrets. She was certain she had made the right decision to bring him home and tend to his injuries. She sensed he was what he said: one of the good guys.

The conviction that she was doing the right thing eased the tension pulling across her shoulders, and she moved farther into the room to unlace his boots, placing them on the floor by the bed, before pulling the duvet over him. Finally, she drew the curtains across the window, and left him to sleep.

Downstairs in the kitchen, she glanced through the window. Her car was right where she had left it outside the garage, now covered in a heavy blanket of snow. She groaned, hesitating in indecision. It was currently blocking her neighbor's access, not that she thought for a second anyone would be driving anywhere in the morning. But still, her conscience wouldn't allow her to leave her car there, not when it might be in someone's way. Forcing herself to make one last effort, she trudged outside to her car and carefully eased it into the garage.

Finally back inside her cottage, now blissfully warm, Willow locked the door, turned out the lights, and crawled into her bed, falling asleep the instant her head touched the pillow.

Chapter Two

Willow stared through the kitchen window, marveling at the amount of snow that had fallen overnight, snow that continued to fall steadily. She had slept well and felt no ill effects from everything that had happened last night. In fact, it could almost have been a dream.

The heavy snowfall had prompted her to call one of her neighbors farther down in the village to check if there was anything she needed, and now she shook her head as she listened to her friend suggesting it was too much trouble to expect Willow to help.

“Honestly, it’s no bother, Gwen.” She smiled into the telephone receiver, her eyes following the path of one particular snowflake as it floated to the ground. “I’ve got to pop into the shop myself anyway, so I can just as easily pick up a few things for you.”

Her attention was caught by the sight of her neighbor, slowly making her way down the garden path next door, with a large basket in her hands. “Just one moment, Gwen.”

She pressed the telephone against her chest, hurried to the back door, and pulled it open to call across the low fence to her neighbor. “Alison! What are you doing? You shouldn’t be outdoors in this; you’re meant to be in bed with the flu.”

Alison White turned with a wan smile; she looked exhausted. "Oh, I'm much…better than I was. I was just…going to get some more logs from the shed. It's fine." The hoarseness of her voice and the pallor of her skin said otherwise.

"No, it isn't fine." A mix of concern and exasperation sharpened Willow's tone. "Go on back inside. Give me five minutes, and I'll pop round and get the logs for you. When is Gary due?"

"He should be back later this afternoon."

"Good. Is your fire already lit? Are you warm enough?" When Alison nodded, Willow smiled. "Okay. Now go on, and I'll be around in a few minutes."

Closing the door and bringing the telephone back to her ear, a sudden prickling sensation at the nape of her neck gave her a moment's warning. She turned to find the stranger standing in the kitchen doorway, leaning against the door jamb. The duffel bag she had brought in from the car last night had obviously contained clothing. He wore clean black jeans, and a navy cotton shirt over the same-colored T-shirt. His short, dark blond hair was slightly spiky on top, as if he had just dragged his hand through it. He was pale and his face taught with pain, but his gaze was sharp and intense.

She gave a nod and a brief smile, aware of a sudden dryness in her mouth. Directing him with a wave of one hand toward the small wooden table and chairs in the middle of the kitchen, she turned back to the phone. "Gwen, I'm sorry. What were you saying? …Oh no, please don't, the snow is far too deep. I'll call in on my way past, pick up your list, and I can take Chappie with me. There's no need for you to go outside."

She paused as Gwen responded. "Good. Now, you've got your heating on and you're warm enough? …Okay, that's good. I'll see you in about an hour. If I'm a little longer, don't start worrying. I've got a couple of things to do first, but I will be around as soon as I can this morning. Is that okay with you? …Right, I'll see you in a bit."

She ended the call and turned around. Her heart skipped a beat when she saw he hadn't moved and still regarded her with that same intense gaze.

"Please. Sit down. I'm really not sure you should be up and about already."

For a moment, she thought he wasn't going to respond, but then he gave a slight shake of his head before moving stiffly to the table and sitting down. His gaze followed her movements as she switched on the kettle, put two slices of bread in the toaster, and poured a glass of water. She placed it in front of him along with a couple of tablets.

"You look like you could do with these; they're just over-the-counter pain killers, I'm afraid. I don't have anything stronger."

He looked down at the tablets before once more resuming his gaze, only this time his eyes, gray she saw now, were curious. "You brought me to your home." His voice was quiet and measured. "I get into your car and hold you at gunpoint, and you bring me to your home." He paused, dropping his head as he blew a long breath out, clearly battling with pain. After a moment, he continued. "You treat my injuries, I'm assuming it was you, and generally act as if I'm your guest?"

Willow spooned instant coffee into two mugs, then added hot water before placing them both on the table alongside a carton of milk. Taking the seat opposite, she drew one mug toward her as he downed the tablets with a long swallow of water.

"I didn't know what else to do." She blew on the hot coffee before taking a sip. "I mean, it wasn't a conscious decision. You told me to drive, and I didn't know where else to take you. You passed out, so I just came home."

He nodded slightly, although his expression told her he wasn't agreeing with her. His gaze really was intense; she found herself unable to look away. "I'd passed out. Why didn't you just dump me at the side of the road, or turn me in to the police?"

She stared at him. "You said no police, no hospitals. And I couldn't just push you out of the car onto the road; I wasn't sure how badly you were hurt."

"I'd just held you at gun point, for Christ's sake." Exasperation finally sharpened his voice, and he checked himself, running a hand across his face. "What's your name?"

Automatically, she smiled and held out her hand. "I'm Willow."

Surprise flickered across his features before a reluctant smile tugged his mouth, causing her breath to catch in her throat. He briefly shook her hand. "Ethan."

"Ethan," she whispered. It was a good name. It suited him. "You told me you were one of the good guys." She traced the grain of the wooden table with her finger. "That's why I didn't turn you in, why I brought you back here."

His jaw dropped, and he ducked his head slightly to better catch her gaze. "And you believed me?"

"Of course, I believed you." She gave a shrug, keeping her gaze firmly on the mug of coffee. "Why wouldn't I? And, besides, you have a good aura."

He gave a short, surprised laugh, shaking his head and leaning back in his chair, flinching as the movement pulled his side. "A good aura. Right."

She pushed her chair back from the table and moved to the counter to butter the hot toast. "Don't knock it. Me believing in your good aura might just have saved your life last night."

Ethan sobered. "I don't doubt it. You might just be my guardian angel."

Willow glanced across at him quickly, trying unsuccessfully to read his expression. She returned to her seat, pushing the plate of toast toward him. "Tuck in. I've had breakfast, and you probably need to eat something."

Regarding her curiously, he took a large bite of toast. "So, tell me. What were you doing parked up in the middle of an industrial estate last night?"

She gave an embarrassed grimace. "I was lost. My friend, Karen, has broken her foot and can't drive, so I offered to drive her son to the train station. I took a couple of wrong turns after dropping him off and got myself completely lost. I'd just pulled over to check the satnav function on my phone when you—"

"When I got into your car and threatened you at gunpoint," he finished for her.

She gave an uncomfortable shrug and lifted a hand to push her long, dark curls behind her ear. As she did so, the sleeve of her jumper fell back to her elbow. Ethan's gaze narrowed on the small cluster of bruises on her forearm, his eyes flicking to hers when she immediately pulled the sleeve down to her wrist. "You didn't mean to."

His eyes widened, and he drew in a sharp breath. "What do you mean? Are you saying I did that?"

She frowned, and shook her head, wafting her hand as if it were of no importance. "It doesn't matter."

His voice, quiet and measured, demanded, "What did I do to you?"

She took another sip from her coffee, deliberately avoiding his gaze, and inwardly cursing herself for saying anything.

"Willow." He waited until she looked at him. "What did I do to you?"

"Nothing. Not really." She stood and began tidying away the breakfast things. "I surprised you, and you reacted instinctively, that's all. It wasn't your fault."

"What. Did I do. To you?"

It was clear he wasn't going to let it go. Dropping the used cutlery in the sink, she gazed through the window, her back to him. "You'd passed out, like I said, and I had to get you into the house. I shook your shoulder to try and wake you."

"And?"

"And…you woke suddenly, grabbed my arm, and pulled me into the car." She closed her eyes. "Then you…you pushed the gun…under my chin."

Behind her, he whispered a soft, explicit curse, and she heard the scrape of the chair as he stood. A moment later, his hands were on her shoulders, gently turning her to face him. His eyes held hers, before dropping to her arm as he carefully pulled the sleeve back to reveal the bruises. His lips tightened as he saw the evidence of his actions, no matter how instinctive.

He brushed his fingers lightly over the bruises before lifting his fingers to her jaw, turning her face to inspect her throat. “I’m so sorry.”

Overwhelmed by his nearness, by the tingling of her skin wherever his fingers touched her, she stepped away. “There’s nothing to be sorry about. Just forget it. Look, I um…I need to get some logs for my neighbor.”

Turning away from him, she pulled on the boots standing behind the door, and fled outside. Gasping in the crisp, chill air, she hurried down the path, blinking in confusion about her unnerving reaction to Ethan’s gentle touch.

Alison had left the log basket by the shed door, and Willow filled it with logs before dragging it slowly back up the garden path, muttering under her breath that she had filled it far too full. However, it did have the positive effect of clearing the path of snow as she hauled it along the paving stones. On reaching the back door, she knocked and went in without waiting for an answer. Heaving the basket over the shallow step into the kitchen, she caught her breath before kicking off her boots and picking up as many logs as she could carry, before going through to the living room. She was relieved to find Alison curled up on the sofa underneath a blanket.

“Ooh, it’s lovely and cozy in here.” Willow carefully stacked the logs on the hearth next to the log burner, then hurried back to the kitchen to bring through the remainder of the logs in the basket.

“Thank you so much, Willow. You really shouldn’t have put yourself out.”

“Nonsense, it’s no bother. I was glad of the distraction to be honest.” She grinned at Alison’s surprised expression and waved her hand to indicate it was of no consequence. “Right, is there anything else you need before Gary gets home?”

Reassured her neighbor was settled and comfortable, Willow let herself out and returned home, hesitating for a moment on the doorstep to take a deep breath. When she pushed open the door, and took off her boots, rubbing her arms to try and get warm, she found Ethan still sitting at the kitchen table. He didn’t speak, and simply watched as she sank into the opposite chair.

She caught his gaze and carried on their conversation as if there had been no interruption. “Now it’s your turn. What were you doing in the industrial estate last night, and who gave you that awful wound?”

His expression instantly became shuttered. It was a long time before he responded. When he did, it was non-committal. “Probably best you don’t know.” He dragged a hand through his hair. “Look, I should go. I know I don’t have any right to ask, but I need your car.”

“Are you serious?”

“I know it’s a lot to ask—”

“That’s not what I mean.” She gestured toward the window. “Have you seen it outside? We only just made it back last night, and it hasn’t stopped snowing since. The village is completely cut off.”

“What?”

He shot from the chair, the sudden movement bringing with it a sharp gasp and leaving him bent over the table, one hand pressed to his side as he breathed through the pain. He waved Willow away as she automatically moved toward him, before heading over to the window. His expression was grim as he viewed the wintry scene. Without a word, he turned and walked through to the living room to pull open the front door.

Beyond her garden, the snow was so deep it was difficult to tell where the pavement ended, and the road began. Perfectly smooth, it was evident no vehicles had passed through. The air was filled with a heavy silence, and the only sound was the rattling chatter of a magpie somewhere close, but the peaceful scene clearly didn't appeal to him.

He turned to her, one hand still pressed against his side. "How far to the nearest main road?"

She shook her head. "It's a good four or five miles. But it's impossible when we've had this much snow."

She gently pushed him to one side and closed the door to prevent the warm air from escaping. "We're right at the bottom of the valley. We get snowed in fairly regularly, I'm afraid."

Ethan paced up and down the small living room, swearing long and impressively fluently. She watched him, faintly amused. "Look, it's fine. You can stay here until the road clears. It's probably a good thing, to be honest, you need to rest. You've lost a lot of blood."

He turned on her. "It's not bloody fine, it's a nightmare. What the hell did you think you were doing, bringing me here into the middle of nowhere?" He spun away from her, breathing harshly.

She stared at his back, stung by his words, irritation spiking through her stomach. "Like I told you before, I didn't know what else to do, but you know what? I'm beginning to think you were right, and I should have just dumped you by the side of the road."

She stalked through to the kitchen and, opening the door to the cupboard under the stairs, took out her coat and put it on, along with her wellington boots. She studiously ignored Ethan when, after a moment, he followed her into the kitchen, and stood watching her.

"I'm sorry, that was unfair."

She didn't answer and concentrated on buttoning up her long, heavy winter coat before pulling the gloves from her pockets and putting those on too. She didn't care if he was sorry.

"I really need to get back…" He stopped and sighed, his head tilted to one side as he levelled that gaze at her.

"What? You need to get back to waving your gun around at more people?" She reached past him into the cupboard to take out a black woolen hat with an oversized fluffy bobble on the top and pulled it over her curls. "Well, as soon as the road clears, you can take my car, okay? And when you do, you can get my wing mirror fixed. I'm assuming it was blown to smithereens by some other guy also waving a gun around?"

He went very still. His face, if it were possible, was even more pale than before, and he simply stared at her.

When he didn't respond, she shrugged and picked up a shoulder bag before throwing open the back door. "I suggest you sit down before you fall down."

****

Ethan stared at the door Willow had not quite slammed behind her. Her throw away comment about the wing mirror left his stomach churning. After waking up to find himself in a strange house, with his wounds tended to, his first and only thought was about how he could get back to York. Her reminder that someone had blown out her wing mirror brought the situation into sharp focus.

He'd known they were close behind him; what if they were close enough to read the car's license plate? He hadn't given a moment's thought to the implications when he saw her car sitting there, had been thinking only of escape, and acted purely on instinct. But in doing so, he had clearly put an innocent bystander in danger. It was going to take Carter no time at all to find out her details from the license plate and then follow them here.

Idiot! He spun away from the door, dragging his hand through his hair. He walked back into the living room, his mind working overtime. Was she an innocent bystander? Her being there last night, in the middle of nowhere, just when he found out someone had double crossed him, was something of a coincidence. And who in their right mind would bring a stranger into their home, especially one who had threatened them at gunpoint? He chewed his lip. It didn't make any sense; none of it made any sense.

Who was she? His gaze swept the room, small and cluttered but tidy. Fairy lights trailed over the mantelpiece and the bookshelves, and he had the impression they were a permanent fixture. She hadn't yet decorated for Christmas. He saw no tree or festive decorations. He stepped closer to the bookshelves lining the wall at either side of the fireplace, scanning the titles. Books were crammed in, filling the shelves until there was no available space left; it was an eclectic mix. Classics were stacked side by side with modern day thrillers, sci-fi and fantasy. One shelf was heaving with books on ancient history, and another full of what he would class as new age mumbo jumbo: spell craft, crystals, homeopathy, and mindfulness.

His attention fell on an ornate chest of drawers standing just inside the doorway to the stairs and kitchen. He moved across to it and hesitated, his fingers tracing the carving on the top, before pulling out one of the drawers. It was filled with candles of various shapes, sizes, and colors. He pulled open another drawer, breathing in a sweet, spicy fragrance as he did so, scented candles and incense. Another drawer was divided into small sections, each one containing different crystals. About to pick up one of the little stones, Ethan hesitated. He had read somewhere once that crystals contained the energy of the owner and were contaminated by someone else's touch.

He frowned and gave a soft laugh; he didn't believe in such things. Nevertheless, he carefully closed the drawer without touching anything. Other drawers contained feathers, ribbons, tarot cards, and a myriad of other trinkets. He stepped away from the chest; it didn't tell him anything about who Willow was, and yet it told him everything he needed to know. It confirmed his instinct. She wasn't involved with Carter; she was who she said she was. In her company for less than an hour this morning, her focus had been on helping others, himself included. And in doing so, she had unwittingly got herself involved in something dangerous.

The nagging pain in his side brought on a new wave of nausea and he sank down into the armchair by the fire to calm his queasy gut. The village was cut off from the main road, which should mean they were safe, for a little while anyway.

He needed to think.

Chapter Three

Willow made her way along the track that ran behind the row of terraced cottages before turning left onto the main street, and the view that had so depressed Ethan minutes earlier. Beyond the hedge and the patchwork fields, rolling hills surrounded the village. The view today was a blinding snow-covered vista, reaching up to meet the pale gray sky, leaden with unshed snow. The *chaca-chaca-chaca* of the magpie still rang out in the stillness. She smiled, her bad temper eased only to be replaced by worry. Ethan was clearly in a lot of pain, and she worried the butterfly strips wouldn't hold, particularly as he didn't seem inclined to sit still.

The deep snow made for heavy going, and she avoided the deeper drifts, picking her way along what she assumed was the path. She chewed her lip, wondering about the man who had burst so suddenly and dramatically into her life. He was clearly in some kind of trouble. And what about his assertion that he was one of the good guys? She sensed this was true, but what did he mean by good guy? Was he with the police? If so, why had he warned her not to take him to the hospital or the police last night?

She gave a sigh, her warm breath mingling with the icy cold air, creating a swirl of circles, before dissipating. There was little point in second guessing who Ethan was, or what trouble he was in. He was here, for now, and no doubt she would find out more in time. The fluttering sensation in the pit of her stomach at the thought of him surprised her, brought the memory of how his nearness, his intense gaze, affected her. She was drawn to him in a way she had never experienced.

"Morning, Willow."

She jumped, and stumbled a little in the snow, so lost in her thoughts she hadn't noticed the man on the opposite side of the road pulling his two children behind him on the bright red, plastic sled. How had she not heard them, laughing, and giggling as they were, and urging their father to go faster?

She smiled and waved as they passed by, and five minutes later she turned off the path, opening the gate to Gwen Matthew's front garden. She had known Gwen all her life, having been her grandmother's best friend but, since Willow's grandmother was no longer with them and with Gwen not having any family living close by, she made a point of keeping in regular touch with the elderly woman.

Gwen opened the door just as she was about to knock, ushering her in and chattering ten to the dozen. Willow allowed herself to be drawn into the quaint old alms-house, sitting down in the warm and cozy living room. Ten minutes later, she was back outside, with Gwen's little Scottie on a lead.

"Come on, Chappie," she encouraged the little dog. "It's not going to be the easiest of walks, I'm afraid, but it saves Gwen from having to take you."

In the end, Chappie coped admirably, having great fun leaping his way through the snow, quite often disappearing into one of the deeper drifts, before reappearing to shake the snow from his face and fur, and generally appearing to have the time of his life as they made their way toward the shop in the middle of the village.

"Jane, am I okay bringing Chappie in with me?" Willow called across to the shopkeeper. "I don't really want to leave him tied up outside in all this snow."

Jane waved a hand. "Yes, of course, no problem. Is Gwen okay?"

"She's fine. I thought I'd save her going out in this."

Slipping the loop handle of Chappie's lead over her arm, she picked up a shopping basket. Millendale's village shop was larger than average, well stocked not only with the usual groceries, but also with various items not usually found in a local shop but which were essential for the camping and walking community who passed through the village in their droves in the summer, and who boosted Jane's income significantly. It was one of the benefits of being part of one of the most popular walking routes in the North of England, known as the Yorkshire Wolds Way.

Willow wandered down the aisle, collecting the bits and pieces Gwen needed, as well as a few items for herself, before stopping at the shelf containing various first aid items. A larger selection than usual was on display in a nod to the passing trade, where the need for first aid was a regular occurrence. She perused the shelf, in her mind's eye seeing Ethan's wound, and hesitantly picked up a box of butterfly strips.

"Morning, Willow."

The voice was close to her ear and she jumped, turning to see a tall, stocky man standing behind her. A black woolen hat was pulled over his dark hair, and the blue padded jacket he was wearing made him appear even larger than usual.

"Heaven's sake, Sam, you made me jump." She smiled at him, and shook her head, dropping the butterfly strips in her basket, along with another packet of sterile dressings.

"Sorry about that." The large grin on Sam Richards' face said otherwise, but his smile faded when he glanced into her basket. "Is everything okay?"

"Everything's fine, thank you." She moved farther along the aisle, once more smiling up at Sam as he walked with her. "Any news from Jonathan? What's the likelihood of him being able to clear the roads, do you think? I'm assuming we're cut off after last night?"

Jonathan Fisher owned the farm at the top of Millendale and, following several years of the village being completely cut off during winter snowfalls, had invested in a snowplow blade that he attached to the front of his tractor. It had been worth the investment, having used the plow to clear the single-track roads into the village more than once.

Sam shook his head. "I spoke to him earlier. He's not going to be able to get out, I'm afraid. There's more snow forecast to come, so I reckon we're on our own for the next few days at least."

She wrinkled her nose. "Yes, I guessed as much."

He looked at her thoughtfully. "You sure you're okay? You know you only need to ask if there's anything I can do."

"I'm fine. Thank you, Sam." She squeezed his arm. "Right, I'd better get these things paid for, and Chappie back to Gwen, or she'll think we've got lost."

He nodded and turned to leave but then swung back. “Oh, I nearly forgot, you are still coming to The Half Moon on Thursday, aren’t you? You know I won’t let a little thing like the village being snowed in stop our Christmas Party.”

She dipped her head with a soft chuckle. “I think the whole village knows that. Yes, I’ll be there.”

Sam raised a hand in farewell as he left the shop, and Willow quickly walked to the till to pay for her groceries. As she left the shop, she saw a familiar figure a little way along the road and hesitated in indecision. Ethan had said no hospitals, no police, but still she worried about his wound. Should she risk it?

****

Walking up the path to her cottage an hour later, Willow thumped her boots on the back doorstep to remove the worst of the snow before kicking them off and leaving them just inside the door. She stood for a moment in the kitchen, listening for any sound of movement, but the house was quiet. After unbuttoning her coat and hanging it in the cupboard, she frowned at the silence. Ethan had been desperate to leave the village, but surely he wouldn’t have been foolish enough to actually attempt it?

She walked through to the living room and stopped in the doorway. He was sitting in her armchair by the log burner, his head resting against the back of the chair with his eyes closed. The light from the window behind him created shadows, emphasizing the planes of his cheekbones and highlighting the darker skin beneath his eyes. In repose he looked younger, more vulnerable somehow.

She caught herself staring and walked into the room to put more logs on the burner. As she straightened, she glanced across to Ethan and gave a start of surprise when she found him awake and watching her.

"Sorry, I didn't mean to wake you."

"You didn't wake me." He carefully eased himself into a more comfortable position. "Did you get Gwen sorted out?"

"Um, yes, I did, thank you." She was momentarily thrown; she hadn't expected him to take in the conversation he had overheard this morning. "It's freezing out there. I was going to make a hot chocolate to warm me up, would you like one?"

"Sounds good."

Returning minutes later with two steaming mugs of hot chocolate, she handed one to him before curling up on the sofa opposite him. Picking up the remote, she switched on the TV as if it were the most natural thing in the world and they were old friends.

"Ooh, *White Christmas*, my favorite." She snuggled deeper into the soft cushions, cupping her hands around the hot mug, and breathing in the sweet chocolatey fragrance.

Ethan laughed softly, bringing his own mug to his lips. "Why am I not surprised?"

"You're not a fan?"

"Can't say I've ever seen it. Not really one for films, in general."

"You've never seen *White Christmas*? I thought everyone had seen it, a bit like the *Wizard of Oz*." Her mouth dropped open when he simply looked at her blankly. "You must have seen that one, surely?"

He stared at her for a beat, and then his face relaxed into a smile. “Okay, yes, I have seen that one.”

She turned her attention back to the film with a smile. “Hmm, not a total loss then.”

“Do you regularly entertain complete strangers in your home?” he asked after a while, his gaze curious.

“No, why?”

He frowned and shrugged. “You appear completely at ease and yet, less than twenty-four hours ago, I was holding you at gunpoint.”

Willow paused. He was right, why was she so sure he meant her no harm? She rarely questioned her instincts and relied on what she sensed about people. In her usual, safe and quiet life, there was little danger in that. But what about now? Was she being foolish?

She looked at him, really looked at him, fully opening her senses and, after a moment, smiled. She sensed his goodness, his strength and warmth. It reaffirmed what she already knew. She trusted him.

Taking a sip of hot chocolate, she looked at him over the rim of the mug. “Should I be worried? Do you mean me any harm?”

“No, of course not. But I’d hardly tell you even if I did, would I?”

“No, but I’d sense it. And I don’t.”

Ethan stared at her. She knew he didn’t understand, but it didn’t matter; few really understood that side of her. People rarely took the time to listen to their feelings and for some reason were more comfortable building up a relationship with their mobile devices.

“Have you got a mobile with you? I’m afraid it’s a bit of a dead zone here. There’s only one network with a reliable signal, and usually only if you're standing by the window."

"I wouldn't expect anything else."

"If you need to get hold of someone, you can use my phone." She decided to ignore his sarcasm. "Or you can use my laptop to send an email?"

He hesitated, running long, slender fingers along his jawline. "I'm not sure…I need to work out a few things first." He looked up quickly. "But thank you. I'm okay for the moment. As you said, maybe I should take it easy for a while, wait until the snow clears."

Willow hid her surprise. He had been desperate to leave earlier. What had happened to change his mind? "Won't someone be wondering where you are?"

She immediately regretted pushing the subject when the shuttered expression once more drew over his face. They sat in growing silence until a sharp rap at the door sounded.

Ethan stiffened immediately. "Are you expecting anyone?"

"Yes, I am, actually."

Lord, he was jumpy. She got up to open the front door, stepping back to let the visitor in. "Laura, thank you so much for coming, I really appreciate it."

"It's no bother." Laura Dennis put down her large leather bag, and eased off her long boots, handing her coat to Willow. "So, where's the patient?"

Ethan got to his feet; his body tensed as if ready for flight. "Willow, what have you done?"

"Will you just relax?" She didn't bother to hide her irritation. "Your wound is really deep, and I'm not a doctor. Laura is. I saw her down in the village earlier and asked for her help."

Laura looked curiously from one to the other. In her mid-forties, her pretty face was framed by a shiny, black pixie cut. "Willow said she thought you might need stitches but can't get you to a hospital. Let's take a look, shall we? Perhaps in the kitchen where there's better light?"

Ethan looked mutinous, and for a moment Willow thought he was going to refuse, but he eventually followed Laura into the kitchen. The two women waited in silence as he painfully shrugged out of his shirt and, after a slight hesitation, started to lift his T-shirt. Willow stepped forward, ready to help ease it over his head.

"Right then," said Laura, briskly. She put her bag on the table and turned him around to get a clear look at the wound on his side. Fresh blood stained the dressing and, as she carefully removed it, saw that only three of the butterfly strips remained in place.

She drew in a sharp breath and stepped back in obvious surprise. She gave Ethan an assessing gaze. "How did you get this wound?"

He remained silent, and simply returned her stare. It was Willow who broke the silence. "Laura, please."

Clearly unhappy, angry even, Laura waved Ethan to a seat before quickly and efficiently attending to the wound. "Well, this is obviously a knife wound, and yes it definitely needs suturing. Willow, you did a lovely job with the butterfly strips, but you were right, they couldn't hold this together."

Ethan hissed as Laura injected a local anesthetic, but she ignored him. His face was turned away, and Willow gazed in fascination at his bare torso, the clearly defined muscles flexing and tensing as he flinched in pain. After waiting a few seconds to allow the local anesthetic to take effect, she proceeded to wash the wound with a saline solution before deftly suturing it closed.

"Willow, are you going to tell me what's going on?" Laura flicked her friend a swift glance before turning back to Ethan as she applied a clean dressing. "I'm not talking to you; you had your chance," she snapped, as he opened his mouth to respond. She directed her attention back to Willow. "Well? Do you know how he got this? Do you even know who he is?"

"He was hurt, and he needed my help."

Laura gave an exasperated sigh. "Willow, you can't help everybody."

"I know. But I could help Ethan. And I trust him."

"Well, you're a fool." Laura closed her eyes for a few seconds before turning to Willow with an apologetic smile. "I'm sorry, I didn't mean that. It's just…this…" She pointed to Ethan's side. "This is serious, honey. And I'm worried about what you might have got yourself into."

"This isn't her fault," Ethan cut in quietly.

Laura favored him with an unfriendly stare before applying a clean dressing to the smaller wound on his shoulder blade, clearly happy with the butterfly strips Willow had applied last night. She stood back with her hands on her hips. "Any other injuries?"

He reached for his T-shirt, the slight smile on his lips belying the pallor of his face. "No. Thank you."

Laura washed her hands in the sink before packing away her things in silence, her movements stiff and angry. Closing her medical bag with a snap, she turned to face them both. "I'm not putting my career on the line for you, Ethan. This is going to be aboveboard, and I shall treat you as an emergency patient, which means I will be registering you as such and recording the treatment undertaken."

She folded her arms across her chest, fixing him with a suspicious gaze, which he returned coolly. "Is Ethan your real name?"

For a moment, he didn't respond, then said, "Ethan McCormick." And carefully pulled on the T-shirt.

"Do you have any identification?"

He leaned back against the kitchen table, an amused smile tugged at his lips. "No."

He flicked a quick glance toward Willow. "I've been working undercover, so the ID I have with me is false. I'd appreciate it if you would hold off writing your report or registering me on the system for a couple of days until I can put a few safety measures in place. For Willow's safety more than anything else."

Laura turned a worried and exasperated glance toward Willow, looking as if she wanted to say more but in the end gave a resigned sigh.

She looked at him with a careful eye. "That's a deep wound, Mr. McCormick. It won't take much to pull those stitches out. Have someone look at them in a week to see how you're doing. I'd like to think you'll be long gone by then, so it won't be me. In the meantime, you need to take it easy and rest."

"So no sledding or making snow angels, then?" He gave a crooked smile. "Thank you. I appreciate your help."

Clearly disarmed, she took a moment to respond. "Willow's judgment is usually sound, so if she says she trusts you… Look, you're welcome. Just don't make me sorry I helped you."

Chapter Four

Ethan was hunched over the table when Willow returned to the kitchen after seeing Laura out. She paused in the doorway. Laura's question about his identify had thrown her; it hadn't occurred to her he might not have given his real name. She gave a mental shrug; "what ifs" didn't help anyone.

She cleared her throat and walked in as Ethan immediately straightened and turned, his chin raised. He pulled his shirt from the back of the kitchen chair.

"I really think you need to get some rest." She smiled, preparing to argue the point. "Doctor's orders."

To her surprise, he closed his eyes briefly and nodded. "I think you're right."

Without a word, she followed him as he made his way up the stairs and into the spare room. He hesitated just inside the door, and she breezed past him to draw the curtains. The duvet was thrown back to one side, revealing the blood-stained blanket, and she pulled it from the bed.

"I'm sorry, I didn't make the bed…" He looked uncomfortable, and Willow gave a soft laugh.

"It's all right. I'll forgive you." She looked around the room, found nothing else out of place. "I'll leave you to it, then. Get some rest."

He moved toward her, his gaze once more intense, searching her face. Hugging the blanket to her chest, she struggled to draw breath, unable to take her eyes from him; she heard nothing above the pounding in her ears when he lifted his hand to gently trace her jawline.

"You're too trusting," he murmured, a slight frown marring his brow.

As if an invisible thread were pulling her, she swayed toward him, and Ethan snatched his hand away, stepping backward as if he'd been stung. Warmth spread across her cheeks and, as he quickly moved to throw his shirt on the bedside chair, she turned away to hide her embarrassment. She had just reached the door when he spoke again.

"Thank you, Willow."

She nodded but didn't turn around and simply pulled the bedroom door closed behind her.

Back downstairs, she picked up the two mugs of hot chocolate, now gone cold, and poured Ethan's down the sink after putting hers in the microwave to warm up again. Grabbing a couple of biscuits, she settled herself on the sofa and flicked through the TV channels until she found the plus-one-hour version of *White Christmas*.

Cradling the hot chocolate in her hands, she tried to concentrate on the film, but her thoughts constantly strayed to Ethan and how much she had wanted him to kiss her. She gave a little giggle, how different from her usual calm, quiet, and predictable life.

Held at gunpoint by an undercover detective, or policeman, or whatever he was, and now harboring him in her little terraced cottage from heaven only knew what. If this had been a film, she would now be in mortal danger herself and in need of protection from the handsome hero. Well, she mused, Ethan was certainly handsome, but this was real life, and she was not in mortal danger, and not in need of protection. From anyone. Her life just wasn't like that.

The familiar, gentle storyline, and songs of the film gradually eased her tumbled thoughts, and she allowed herself to become engrossed, sipping her hot chocolate and nibbling the biscuits. When the film ended, she gave a satisfied sigh and stretched her arms above her head. There hadn't been a sound from the spare room above, and she assumed Ethan was asleep. Glancing at the clock, she realized it was well into the afternoon and set about warming up some soup.

Ten minutes later she stood outside the spare room, listening for any sounds to indicate he might be awake. All was silent, so she carefully pushed open the door and peered inside. He was sleeping and didn't stir when she moved into the room to place the tray, containing a flask of soup and a couple of bread rolls wrapped in tinfoil, on the bedside table.

****

Having finished her own soup, Willow stood for a while watching the snow spiraling down from the sky, as always marveling at the view from her home. Her living room looked out over open countryside, the fields on the opposite side of the road rising to the high hills of the valley, the view today full of muted blues and grays through the falling snow. Cold radiated from the window, and she shivered, moving once more to the warmth of the log burner.

Picking up the remote control for the television, her fingers hovered over the buttons, focusing on the weather presenter's forecast on the local news.

"The winter storm is set to continue, as a north-westerly weather front hits the UK. Overnight we will see temperatures drop once more as an active frontal system moves into our area, bringing with it strong gale force winds and heavy snow tomorrow."

The presenter gave a sympathetic smile. *"There is a good chance that some rural communities could be cut off. Power cuts are likely, and other services, such as mobile phone coverage, could be affected. It's batten down the hatches time for some, I'm afraid. However, the storm is expected to move across fairly quickly, with slightly higher temperatures expected later on Tuesday, and gradually increasing over the next few days."*

"What do you mean, *could be cut off?*" Willow muttered. "We already are."

She frowned, glancing through the window once more. She loved the snow, but a winter storm was something different; she wasn't keen on the wind, didn't like the destruction it caused. With a worried sigh, she switched to a Christmas music channel and stood in front of the log burner, gazing around her small living room with a critical eye and wondering what Ethan thought of it.

Floor to ceiling bookshelves lined the alcoves at either side of the fireplace, crammed with books, and anything else she was able to squeeze in. Candles and crystals covered every available surface, and a smile curved her lips as her gaze fell on her favorite piece of furniture, the heavy, intricately carved antique chest of drawers.

Each drawer was a different shape and size, her very own cabinet of curiosities containing myriad bits of ribbon, crystals, incense, oils, and anything else she needed to make her charms. Cluttered, her mother called this room; Willow preferred the term cozy. She had a feeling Ethan would probably agree with her mother. She shrugged. Her house, her rules.

Rummaging through the cabinet, she gathered ribbon, cloves, oils, and scissors, and some oranges from the fruit bowl. For the next hour, she sang away softly to the music and lost herself in making the beautifully scented Christmas decorations she loved.

Ethan was still asleep when she brought up another tray for him, this time with a sandwich and a flask of tea. He had obviously woken at some point because the flask of soup was empty and the bread had been eaten.

She took a moment to place the little recovery charm she had made for him over the bed post before removing the empty tray and retreating from the room. He didn't stir for the rest of the evening. At ten o'clock, Willow turned off the television and went to bed.

****

Ethan woke with a start, sitting bolt upright in the bed and gasping as pain lanced through his side. Momentarily disoriented, he blinked away the fading memory of the dream that had woken him, a replay of Taylor thrusting the knife toward him, catching him by surprise. In his dream, he had felt the knife slip deep between his ribs, had seen the triumph in Taylor's eyes as the knife pierced his heart. In reality, he'd thrown himself sideways, away from the gleaming blade, and had felt only a momentary sting as the knife sliced through his side in a glancing blow rather than the fatal thrust that had been intended.

He blew out a breath, shaking his head to rid himself of the last remnants of the dream, and frowned as he gazed about him. It had grown dark while he slept, and the room was now lit by the soft glow of the bedside lamp. The soup he had eaten earlier on waking had been replaced by a round of sandwiches, and his stomach rumbled at the thought of food. He eased himself back against the pillows and reached for the flask of tea to pour himself a cup.

The room was warm, the bed comfy, and the food and drink welcome. He became aware of a fresh citrus fragrance mingled with a woodsy, spicy scent, and as he looked around for the source noticed the clove-studded orange hanging on the bedpost, and which hadn't been there previously.

Willow.

It had been a long time since anyone had shown such care and kindness toward him, and he wondered at his luck in finding her last night. He had no doubt she had saved his life.

He took a bite of the sandwich. Someone had betrayed him, told Carter that he was working undercover. He, Danby, and Taylor had been sent out on a job, or so he had thought. But something about the men's demeanor had set his instincts on edge when they arrived at his flat to pick him up. Something wasn't right. They were trying to act normally, but their good humor was forced, and Ethan had known immediately his cover had been blown. He kept up the charade, carried on as normal, but picked up his duffel bag as they left the flat and slung it casually over his shoulder. He was going to have to take his chance when it came and needed to be prepared.

Walking into the deserted warehouse, the two men had hung back a little, and as Ethan turned toward them he had seen Danby reaching for his gun. Ethan had reacted immediately, instinctively, moving like lightning to snatch the weapon from Danby before he realized what was happening.

Now in possession of the gun, from the corner of his eye he had seen Taylor lunging toward him. Throwing himself to the side, Ethan hadn't been quick enough to avoid the knife completely, had felt the sting of the blade. He kept moving, using Taylor's momentum to push him into Danby. The two men had fallen in a confused heap, and Ethan had made his escape, noting movement on the stairwell above: more of Carter's men.

He burst out of the building and saw a solitary car standing on the tarmac with the engine idling. Without thinking, he had flung open the door and got in, hoping it wasn't more of Carter's men but prepared to pull the trigger if it was.

Ethan closed his eyes. It hadn't been Carter; it had been his guardian angel.

****

"So that's the main road out of the village?"

Ethan frowned at the narrow road meandering away from the village. The snow had drifted high up against the hedges, making the road appear even more narrow than it really was. It was patently obvious no vehicle, snowplow or not, was getting through.

Willow nodded and, as he turned back toward the village, fell into step beside him. She cast him a surreptitious glance as they walked together in silence; her brother's thick, navy parker coat suited Ethan. Now living in Australia, Patrick kept a few items of clothing at her house, mainly the heavier winter clothing he didn't want to carry back and forth whenever he visited, which wasn't often but usually around Christmas. She had lent Ethan one of his jumpers and his coat, and although Patrick was slightly heavier set than Ethan, the jumper and coat fit well enough.

"What about the fields? Any public footpaths or rights of way, other ways to get into the village?"

She frowned. "I'm assuming you mean generally rather than now when the weather's bad? Well, there's the Yorkshire Wolds Way walk that passes through the very end of the village. We get a lot of business in the village from walkers, mainly in the summer, but there's no way anyone could come in through there or across the fields, not when the snow is this bad."

She glanced across at him once more as they walked past the row of terraced cottages where she lived. "Tell me again why you need a tour of the village."

"I just want to get a feel for the place," he shrugged, his gaze taking in his surroundings. "Get my bearings."

Unconvinced, Willow sensed there was more to it but couldn't think what. She decided not to push it. It was taking all her concentration to trek through the deep snow that was significantly deeper than yesterday when she had walked down to the shop. She wore her customary long, full skirt with her wellington boots, which didn't make walking through snow particularly easy.

Ethan had cast an odd glance at the skirt but had the good grace to keep silent when they had left the house. They hadn't seen anyone else out on their walk, and it didn't take much imagination for her to believe they might be the last people on Earth following some dreadful apocalyptic event. She giggled at such fantastic thoughts, and Ethan looked across at her, his eyebrows raised.

"Sorry, I was just thinking this is like something from a disaster film, and we're the only survivors." When he didn't respond, just gave her the usual stare, she carried on. "You know, it's so quiet, no one else is around."

His only response was a slight nod, and she suppressed another giggle. "Of course, that requires an imagination."

"Are you suggesting I don't have any?" He carried on walking, looking straight ahead, his expression deadpan.

She looked up in surprise. Did he just make a joke?

He drew to a halt as they approached the middle of the village, his gaze taking in the little village green with its Christmas tree in the middle and the road that branched left and right. The Half Moon pub and the village shop stood on the far side of the snow-covered green, with pretty, terraced houses lining the road. To her it was a picture-perfect scene, particularly with the snow, but Ethan's expression told her he was seeing something different. He stood for a moment, taking everything in, and she tried to see it from his point of view, as a stranger might see it, as he was seeing it. She shook her head; to her, it was still a pretty village scene, but his gaze was assessing and watchful.

"Are you looking for something?"

He didn't answer immediately and pointed to where the road branched off. "Do both roads take you out of the village?"

"No, just the one on the right. It's like the one at the other end of the village, past my house, fairly narrow and winding. It takes you through a few villages, but after seven or eight miles it brings you to the main road."

She turned to point along the other road, but her foot caught in the thick snow. She stumbled forward, grasping the front of Ethan's coat to prevent herself from falling. He caught her arms to steady her, hissing in pain as the movement obviously pulled his stitches.

"Oh gosh, I'm sorry." She looked up in embarrassment but drew in a sharp breath when she realized how close he was.

It had started snowing again, and she was near enough to see droplets of snow melting on his eyelashes. The intensity of his gaze, the feeling of his fingers curled tightly around her upper arms, left her breathless and unable to move. Her lips parted, but she couldn't think of a thing to say when his gaze immediately dropped to her mouth. Electricity sparked between them, and her heart thumped even harder against her chest as he drew her a few millimeters closer. His eyes flicked back to meet hers, his expression unreadable, and then he very slowly, very gently pushed her away from him.

The spell broken, Willow released her grip on his coat and stepped back with a little, self-conscious laugh. "I maybe should have said I'm fairly clumsy." She straightened her hat and cleared her throat. "Well, as I was going to say. That road there leads up to Jonathan Fisher's farm. It's a dead end, but you can also link to the Yorkshire Wolds Way walk up there."

"And there are no other roads into the village, apart from the two you've shown me?"

"No." She pulled her coat a little tighter around her as she noticed the wind was picking up. "So, what next? I can take you round the back of the village to the school and the village hall, but there are no other roads out of the village. We can do if you want, though. Get my steps up."

Again, that stare, that silence.

"Steps. You know, ten thousand steps a day minimum…" She sighed at his lack of response. He really was hard work.

But then he quirked the corner of his mouth, and it made her stomach quiver. "I know what you meant."

"Oh. I…um—"

"You're a funny girl, Willow." His voice was soft, almost lost in the wind.

Her mouth dropped open. "Oh," she said again. "Funny ha ha, or funny weird?"

His smile slowly broadened, lighting up his eyes, and despite the snow now falling heavily and the growing wind, a warm glow spread over her. He didn't respond, but as a particularly strong gust of wind rocked them he turned away to frown at the dark sky in the distance and the low growl of the wind.

"I think maybe we ought to get back. It looks like the storm is almost here."

Chapter Five

As the storm continued to batter the cottage, Willow voiced her worries about how Gwen was coping. Just a few minutes ago, after the storm took out the electricity—as predicted yesterday—she announced her intention to go down to Gwen's.

"You can't stop me," she said, quietly determined. "Gwen doesn't have anyone here. She's alone."

"What about her neighbors?"

She shook her head. "They're away for the winter, and those on the other side wouldn't think to check. I'm going, Ethan, whether you like it or not."

He slowly turned toward her. "Guardian angel," he murmured, shaking his head. His eyes dropped from her face to her jumper, to the long, heavy skirt that reached to her toes. "You need to change; you'll trip over in that, and God knows we're going to find it difficult enough as it is. Do you have any trousers? Jeans?"

"Of course, I do. Wait, what do you mean *we*? Are you coming too?"

"Well, I'm not going to let you go out in that alone, am I?" He walked toward the kitchen. "We need candles, matches, food possibly. Do you have a backpack?"

****

Ten minutes later, Ethan shrugged the backpack over his shoulders and turned a critical glance toward

Willow as she stood there in jeans and boots, muffled up in her heavy winter coat, hat, scarf, and gloves. "Okay, let's go."

"Ethan, I'm not sure you should come. Laura was clear you needed to rest. Your wound is deep, and you lost a lot of blood. I know the walk this morning really took it out of you." She bit her lip. "Maybe you should stay here."

He hitched the backpack a little higher. "I'm coming with you."

She pulled open the front door and stepped outside, but no sooner had they left the shelter of the house than the full force of the storm hit them. She was immediately shaken by the strength of the wind already threatening to knock her from her feet and was sure the only reason she hadn't fallen already was due to the deep snow lending some stability to her footing. The wind howled around them, and she put her hands over her ears, frightened by the awful sound. She closed her eyes against the sharp, icy flakes of snow lifted by the wind and thrown forcefully into her face. Ethan's hands gripped her shoulders, and she jumped, opening her eyes to see his face inches from hers.

"Come on, we need to move," he shouted over the wind. "You'll be okay."

She hadn't realized the strength of the storm or the disabling impact of fear. She forced her feet to move when Ethan took her hand and pulled her with him.

There had been several more inches of snow just since this morning, and it was a stark contrast to the calm and peaceful walk she had enjoyed yesterday on her way to Gwen's house. Today the sky was gunmetal gray, crowding in on them oppressively, and bringing with it an eerie sense of danger. Now more than ever it didn't take any imagination to believe this was a post-apocalyptic world.

It was darkening rapidly, despite it only being mid-afternoon, and she struggled to draw breath as the wind continued to batter them. Stumbling in a particularly deep snow drift, she was an easy target for the next vicious blast of wind and fell face forward into the snow.

She lay there in shock for a few seconds before scrambling to her feet, Ethan's hand under her arm steadying her when she would have fallen once more.

"You okay?" The wind tore the words from his mouth, but she understood his meaning.

She nodded, her face stinging from where her cheek had broken through the thin crust of snow. She looked up at him, saw his eyes widen at the sight of something over her shoulder. Reaching for her, he pulled her into his arms and twisted, shielding her with his body from whatever it was he had seen as they fell into the snow. The weight of his body on hers winded her, and she struggled to draw breath. Unable to get the air she needed, Willow shook her head wildly in panic, and he immediately rolled onto his side.

"That was too bloody close." He brushed the hair from her face as he squinted to check she was okay before closing his eyes and falling back against the snow, blowing out a long, relieved breath.

"What was it?"

Ethan lay still for another few seconds before getting to his feet and reaching for her hand. He looked along the road, seeming to search for something, then pointed to an object stuck in a snowdrift farther down the road.

A triangular road sign, shaken loose by the fierce wind, listed drunkenly to one side.

"Oh, my God!"

His face was grim. "Like I said, we need to move. Quickly."

It was another five minutes before they made it to Gwen's house, and Willow had never been more relieved. Her hands were close to frozen from the sodden gloves as a result of several more falls into the snow. She also had a sore neck from constantly looking over her shoulder, half expecting to be hit by more flying debris.

"It's me, Willow." She thumped on the door, half shielded by Ethan crowding in on her as they sheltered from the worst of the wind. "Gwen, please open the door."

The door opened, and they stumbled in, almost knocking her friend over in the process. "Willow!" She stepped back from the door, her hand against her chest. "Oh, my goodness."

"I'm so sorry. It's a little bit windy out there," Willow gasped, managing a light laugh and steadying herself against the wall as Ethan pushed the door shut on the storm outside. "We just wanted to make sure you were okay."

The old woman didn't speak for a moment, and the fingers she held against her cheek were trembling slightly. "Oh Willow, you shouldn't have come out in this storm. But I'm so thankful you did. I…"

She broke off on a sob and turned her face away, clearly embarrassed. Chappie was fussing around the two visitors, and she bent down to hide her distress, patting the little dog and attempting to calm him.

"Come on now, Chappie. It's Willow and her friend, and we're very happy to see them, aren't we?"

"Oh sorry, this is Ethan," said Willow, quickly. "He's a…um, he's a friend who's staying with me."

"Good to meet you." He blew on his hands and frowned when he took in the coat and gloves Gwen was wearing. "You weren't planning on going out in the storm, I hope?"

"Oh, no." Her voice quivered. "It's just, I've no heating or electricity and the fire's gone out; I couldn't get to the shed for more logs, and I was so cold."

"Oh Gwen." Willow hugged the old woman. "Come on, let's get you sorted."

They went through to the living room, and Willow grimaced. It was freezing without the fire and no heating, and as she breathed out, her breath swirled in the chill air. The two small tealight candles on the mantelpiece barely penetrated the gloom. No wonder her friend was so distressed.

"Right, Willow, you light some more candles, and I'll go and get the logs," Ethan said, taking charge immediately. He went through to the kitchen, returning quickly. "Gwen, I see you have a gas cooker? How about you heat up some water to make us a hot drink?"

Gwen's worried expression cleared, and she nodded immediately, clearly grateful to be doing something, and went through to the kitchen.

"Thank you," said Willow softly.

"She'll be okay." He touched her cheek. "I'll get the logs." He disappeared into the kitchen, and she heard the back door opening and closing as he went into the back garden. A few minutes later he returned carrying an old metal bucket.

"I found some kindling and coal in the shed." He bent stiffly to place the bucket on the hearth. When he straightened, he blew out a breath and rested a hand on the mantelpiece. "Are you okay to get the fire started while I fetch the logs?"

His face was pale, and Willow touched his arm. "Why don't you stay here, and I'll get the logs?"

"No, no it's fine." He was already halfway to the kitchen, and when he returned five minutes later with an armful of logs, the living room was looking decidedly more cheerful with the many candles Willow had lit, and the fledgling fire was just taking the edge off the chill air.

By the time he had retrieved a third armful of logs, leaving them in a shopping bag by the back door, the fire was snapping and crackling cheerily, throwing out a good deal of warmth.

Gwen appeared from the kitchen carrying a tray with three mugs and a plate of biscuits and placed it on the coffee table in the middle of the room. She glanced behind her toward the kitchen before moving closer to Willow.

"Is Ethan all right? He seems to be in a bit of pain."

Willow cast a swift glance toward the doorway but gave a bright smile. "He's fine. He slipped and fell on the way here; well, that's to say I slipped and fell and managed to drag him down with me too, and he landed awkwardly. He's just winded, that's all, nothing serious."

Gwen seemed to accept her explanation, and as she settled down into the armchair Willow went through to the kitchen.

She hesitated in the doorway. Ethan was hunched over the kitchen sink, his head bowed.

"Are you okay?"

He straightened immediately and turned to her with a tight smile. "I'm fine. Just a little sore. Painkillers should kick in soon."

He gingerly shrugged out of his jacket, hanging it over the back of a kitchen chair before following her back into the living room. He sank into the armchair by the fire. "How are you doing, Gwen? Are you warmer?"

The old woman smiled. "Oh yes, thank you. I'm much better now." She looked around the room, now more cozy and lit by the warm fire. "You even thought to bring scented candles, Willow. You're so kind. And thank you for the pomander, it smells just like Christmas."

"Oh, you know me," she responded with a smile. "I have enough candles to start my own shop. I just grabbed a handful from my Christmas box, thought it might cheer you up a little. And you're welcome to the pomander; I made a few last night."

"Did you run out of red ribbon?" Ethan asked curiously.

She followed his gaze to the clove studded orange hanging from the mantelpiece. "Run out of ribbon? What do you mean?"

"It's just that one is the same as all the ones you've got hanging in your living room, with a red ribbon. The one you hung in my room had a gold ribbon." He shrugged. "I just wondered."

"Oh, well these are just decorations for Christmas. Yours is…well, yours is a healing, recovery charm so it was a little different. Gold ribbon, as you say, and frankincense."

He stared at her thoughtfully, but his gaze swung to Gwen when she spoke. "Willow's very clever, you know. She's always making people little charms and things."

"Is she now?"

The three of them fell into silence, safe and warm in the cozy living room as the wind continued to howl around the house. It rattled the windows, causing the curtains to flutter as it found its way in through the frames. Suddenly, Chappie started barking and growling, running between the door to the hallway and the window.

Gwen gave a cry of alarm. "Oh Chappie, please stop it." She plucked at the sleeve of her jumper in agitation, looked to Willow and Ethan for reassurance. "He's been doing that all day. I hate it when he barks at nothing; it frightens me."

"Chappie!" The dog stopped immediately at Ethan's sharp command, probably more from surprise than obedience. He patted the side of his chair. "Come here and settle down."

With a final gruff bark, Chappie trotted over to Ethan and settled himself at his feet. "The wind is carrying all sorts of debris with it, it'll be branches and stuff like that being tossed around, that's all." His voice was calm and reassuring. "There won't be anyone out there today, believe me."

Gwen lifted her chin with quiet dignity. "You must think me a rather pathetic old woman, Ethan."

"I don't think anything of the sort."

"Believe it or not, I didn't used to be frightened of a thing". She smiled wistfully, her faded blue eyes distant with memories. "I used to work for a hugely successful businessman and traveled the world with him." She gave a giggle. "Oh, he used to get himself into all sorts of scrapes, let me tell you. Of course I was the one who got him out of them!"

Ethan settled back in his chair and smiled. "Tell me about them."

Willow watched as he chatted with her friend. *She's falling under his spell, too.*

She knew he was engaging Gwen in conversation to take her mind off the storm, but as she talked about her career her friend became more animated than she had seen her in a long time. The room was so familiar to Willow, but she had never really taken a great deal of notice of the many photographs and ornaments dotted around. Now, as she looked around her and took more notice, she felt the weight of nostalgia, of the life Gwen had lived, the places she had traveled. Her fingers were laden with old fashioned gold rings that spoke of the fashion of the time when she was in her twenties and thirties. Willow imagined the care and love with which they had been chosen, perhaps by her late husband, Bill.

What tales would she have to tell when she grew older, she wondered. Soothed by the soft murmur of their voices and the warmth of the room, her eyes grew heavy and without realizing she was falling, drifted off to sleep.

"Come on sleepyhead, wake up."

She awoke with a start, opening her eyes to see Ethan crouched down by her chair and laughing softly as he caught her hands in his. "Hey, I'm sorry. I didn't mean to startle you."

She couldn't speak, was overwhelmed by the feelings this man stirred in her, and she looked down at her hands lying in his, fascinated by the tingling sensation his touch generated.

He straightened, and she resisted the urge to tighten her fingers but instead allowed him to pull away. "Come on, we've made tea."

She dropped her legs to the floor and sat up a little straighter, rubbing the sleep from her eyes as Gwen came through from the kitchen with two dishes piled high with pasta. She handed one to Willow before taking her seat by the fire.

"Your young man is pretty handy in the kitchen, I must say," she said, with some satisfaction. "Not like my Bill."

"I've a feeling Ethan is probably pretty handy at most things," she muttered, digging her fork into the pasta. She looked up quickly as he walked in with his own bowl of pasta, his raised eyebrow indicating he had heard. She looked away, warmth flaring across her cheeks.

Gwen looked at her. "What did you say, dear?"

"Oh, nothing." She concentrated on her food. "This looks lovely, thank you. You should have woken me."

"Nonsense." Gwen took a mouthful of pasta, savoring the taste before continuing. "Besides, Ethan said it was time someone looked after you for once, and I agreed with him."

His expression was unreadable in the flickering candlelight, and after a moment Willow dropped her gaze and they ate their tea in companionable silence.

****

"Are you sure you're going to be all right here?" Gwen looked between Ethan and Willow with a worried expression.

"We'll be fine," he reassured her. "Willow can have the sofa, and I'll take the armchair. Believe me, I've slept on worse."

After they had cleared away their evening meal, Gwen had nervously peered through the curtains as the darkness fell and reluctantly suggested it was time they were getting back to Willow's. Her relief had been palpable when Ethan calmly told her they would stay the night. Her next worry had been to wonder where they would sleep in her one bedroomed alms-house, but Willow reassured her they would be fine in the living room. Gwen had once more settled down, and they had spent an enjoyable evening playing cards.

As the evening drew to a close, Willow went through to the bedroom, putting a couple of hot water bottles in the bed and piling on more blankets to ensure Gwen would be warm enough through the night.

She was just closing the bedroom door when a terrifyingly loud groaning sound, loud enough to be heard over the wind, stopped her in her tracks. It had come from outside. There was a second of stillness and then an almighty crack, and Willow ran through to the living room. Gwen turned to her with frightened eyes.

"Where's Ethan?"

Before Gwen could respond, she heard the back door being pulled open and hurried through to the kitchen to see him standing in the doorway, looking out into the darkness.

"Ethan, what was it?"

“I don’t know. I can’t see anything.” He shook his head and after a moment closed the door, ushering her back into the living room. “My best guess is that a tree has come down in the storm, but I don’t think it’s close enough to have done any damage to the surrounding houses. I don’t know, it might have been anything.”

Willow started walking swiftly to the door but halted as he caught her arm.

“Hey, hey, where are you going?”

“We need to find out what that noise was. We need to do something.” She shifted from one foot to the other, full of nervous energy, her eyes darting from Ethan to Gwen.

He caught her hands in his, holding them against his chest as he ducked his head to look into her eyes. “We can’t go out in this, okay? You know that.”

“But what if—”

“But nothing,” he said firmly. “It’s pitch black out there, you know how dangerous it is. I couldn’t hear anything, there were no voices, no sign of any fire. I’m sure no one was hurt by anything. I’ll check it out in the morning, okay?”

“He’s right,” Gwen said in a surprisingly strong voice. “It might have been one of the trees surrounding the school playing field.”

“Oh, of course.” Her shoulders sagged in relief. “Yes, that must be it. And if it is, then it will have fallen onto the field. It won’t have damaged anything. That’s most likely it, isn’t it?” She looked up at Ethan, her hands still clasped in his against his chest, her eyes imploring him to reassure her.

“I don’t know, Willow,” he said, honestly. “But yes, it’s likely. It sounded like a tree coming down, but I didn't hear anything else. I'm sure if it had come down on a building or something like that there would be a lot of activity."

She nodded.

"Okay?" He waited until she looked up at him before giving her hands one last squeeze and stepping away from her. "Okay, one more round of cards, and we'll call it a night."

Chapter Six

It was too cold for Chappie in the bedroom, and he was curled up in front of the fire, fast asleep as Ethan threw on another log before joining Willow on the sofa. He leaned his head back, closing his eyes for a moment before turning his head to look at her. She was sitting sideways facing him, her legs pulled up to her chest and her head resting on the back of the sofa.

"Hell of a few days," he said softly as he searched her face. "Tell me, Willow. What do you do?"

"For a job, you mean? I teach at the primary school in the village."

With a quiet laugh he ran a hand across his face, his fingers rasping against the stubble. "Of course, you do."

"Are you laughing at me?" Confused and a little hurt, she looked away from him.

"No." He reached across to cup her face gently with his hand. "I'm not laughing at you. It's just…it's just exactly the kind of job I imagined you to have." He traced her lips with his thumb, drawing in a quick breath as her lips parted slightly. His expression changed, became serious, and he frowned as if unable to work her out. "You're too good to be true. How can anyone be so good?" he murmured.

Her lips burned from his touch, and she covered his hand with hers, turning her head to press her lips against his palm, blinking in surprise when he immediately pulled his hand away. She shrank back into the sofa, dropping her feet to the floor and turning to face the fire, closing her eyes in mortification, recognizing that once again he had made it clear he wasn't seeking closeness. How had she misread the signals so completely? Did he not feel the same pull?

"Willow." He reached for her, but she got to her feet, and stepped toward the fire with her back to him.

"I'm sorry. I…I guess I misread you." She heard him move, felt him standing close behind her much as he had done yesterday, and closed her eyes when he ran his hands down her arms before turning her to face him.

"You didn't misread me," he said, frowning. "I think we both know I'd be lying if I said I didn't feel it too."

"Then why do you pull away as if you can't bear me to touch you?"

"Because you make me feel out of control."

She blinked in surprise. "I do?"

He smiled then and gently brushed the hair from her cheek before tipping her face to his. "Yes, you do. Very much so."

He was so close, his gaze intense and hungry, and she held her breath, desperately wanting to lift her lips to his but sensing his withdrawal if she did.

"Ethan," she whispered.

He gave the slightest shake of his head, but after a moment brushed his lips against hers as if unable to help himself. It was just the slightest butterfly touch, but it stilled the breath in her throat, her lips tingled, and she lifted her gaze to his.

She reached up to trace his jaw with her fingers and saw his eyes close, sensed the inner battle he was fighting with himself as he bent his head once more and kissed her. This time there was no tentative exploration, this time Ethan kissed her as if he couldn't get enough of her, one hand buried in her hair, the other trailing down her spine, his fingers splayed over the small of her back, pulling her into him and leaving her in no doubt how much he wanted her. Willow was lost, her senses overwhelmed as she wrapped her arms around his neck and kissed him back. All too soon he was pulling away, shaking with the effort it took to regain control as he rested his forehead against hers, his breath coming in harsh gasps.

He gave a soft laugh, his lips curving into a crooked smile as he took a step back, his hands sliding down her arms to gently clasp her fingers. "You definitely make me feel out of control."

"Is that so bad?"

"Now? Here? Yes, it is so bad. I can't risk…" He hesitated, obviously changing what he had been about to say. "I need to stay focused, it's not why I'm here."

He returned to his seat on the sofa, and after a moment she joined him, turning to face him and hugging a cushion to her.

"Why are you here?"

"Because I passed out in your car and you brought me here in the middle of a snowstorm."

"That's not what I meant, and you know it." She wasn't going to let him off the hook this time. "And don't fob me off with the 'it's better if you don't know' rubbish."

"It's not rubbish, Willow, it's—"

"I don't care," she interrupted. She leaned forward to grasp his arm. "Ethan, what happened to you? You told Laura you were working undercover, so what happened? Who gave you that awful wound? Who were you running from?"

She let the silence grow, refusing to give in, and saw his expression shift from irritation to uncertainty as he pondered her question.

"I don't know," he said, eventually. "I've been working undercover for six months and was close to being able to bring them in, and then… I don't know. Something. Someone."

"Someone what? Someone found out?" She looked at him, her eyes widening when he simply looked at her. "You mean someone betrayed you?"

His expression was grim. "I don't know. I've been trying to work it out. I can't think of any other explanation. Nothing else makes any sense."

"Who would do that? Why would anyone do that?"

He gave a humorless laugh. "There are a lot of reasons why someone would do that." He looked at her, and his face relaxed. "Not everyone is like you."

"Don't say that," she snapped, angrily. "I'm not this…this saint you seem to think I am."

"I don't think you're a saint." He smiled, reaching out to give her hair a gentle tug. "But you are the kindest, most thoughtful, gentle person I've ever met."

"Clearly you're not mixing with the right people," she said grumpily, refusing to be charmed by him.

"I think that's a pretty fair assessment." His soft laughter broke through her reserve, and she gave a reluctant smile.

Willow looked at him in the flickering firelight, at the shadows beneath his eyes, the lines around his mouth. "I know you don't like me asking, but how are you doing? You've hardly been following doctor's orders and resting today. I don't think you realize just how much blood you lost." She bit her lip. "Have you checked your stitches?"

What if he had pulled them open? She doubted Gwen had anything more than a basic first aid kit.

"Is this an excuse to get me to take my shirt off?" He laughed softly as color rose in her cheeks, and he shook his head. "I'm joking. I'm fine, don't worry."

"But you know what Laura said." Her face was burning, and she kept her gaze firmly on her hands folded in her lap. "You weren't quite doing snow angels but—"

"But I was in the snow with an angel," he said, quietly. Again, he cut her off when she opened her mouth to negate his words. "Will you stop? I'm fine. I've checked the stitches. They're sore, but they're holding, okay?"

"Well, at least it sounds as if the storm is easing," she said after a while. "They said on the news that it's meant to get warmer over the next few days, so hopefully the roads should clear fairly soon. You won't be stranded here for much longer."

"And you'll be able to get back to normal, have the house to yourself again," agreed Ethan. He looked at her, his head on one side as a sudden thought struck him. "Do you have someone special, Willow? Someone in your life?"

She stared at him, offended. "Do you think I'd kiss you like that if I did?"

He gave a soft chuckle and held his hands up in mock surrender. "I don't know, maybe. I was just asking."

"Well, no, I don't." She huffed a little, flexing her shoulders uncomfortably. "There was for a while, but it didn't really work out. I'm happy as I am for now. If someone comes along, they come along, if they don't, they don't."

"From what little I've seen, I can't imagine there are too many opportunities to meet someone new in a small village like this?"

Willow shrugged, unconcerned. "There are always opportunities. I'm not in any rush." She turned her gaze on him, watching the shadows play across the planes of his face in the flickering firelight. "What about you? Do you have anyone?"

He was watching the flames and wrinkled his nose in response. "No. The kind of job I do doesn't really lend itself to a relationship. Not for me, anyway. It's not fair on the person I'm with, or on me." He gave a thoughtful half-smile. "She would always be worrying if I was okay, if I was going to come home. And me, well, I'd be worrying about her worrying. I wouldn't be able to do the things I do without thinking. I'd always be unconsciously second guessing the risk, asking what ifs. I couldn't do my job."

"It sounds lonely," she whispered.

Ethan didn't respond, and they sat in silence, both lost in thought until after a while he carefully covered her with a blanket, blew out the candles, and settled down in the armchair and closed his eyes. Willow watched him in the warm firelight until her eyes grew heavy, and she fell asleep.

****

Willow opened her eyes, shut them, and opened them again, blinking a few times to try and bring into focus the unfamiliar, blurry view just a few inches from her nose. Why was she looking at a swirl of green and red velour? She squeezed her eyes shut again, willing away the last vestiges of sleep. Of course, the storm, Gwen's house…that kiss. Her eyes flew open, and she struggled to free one arm from the blanket, turning away from the multi-colored back of the sofa and shuffling around to face the room. She stilled immediately at the sight of Ethan sitting in the armchair, looking across at her.

"Hey, good morning."

"Morning." She dipped her head and ran her hand self-consciously over her sleep tousled hair. Heavens, she must look a sight. Glancing at her watch, she saw it was just past eight o'clock and sank back against the cushions.

When he disappeared into the kitchen with a knowing smile, she flung aside the blanket and hurried into the bathroom. Emerging a few minutes later, having done her best to look presentable, she returned to find Ethan back in the armchair and a plate of toast and a mug of coffee waiting for her.

"Thank you. You didn't have to."

He shrugged. "My pleasure. Did you sleep well?"

"I did, actually." She nibbled at the slice of toast, tucking her legs beneath her on the sofa. "How about you?"

He grimaced, running a hand across his jaw. "I've slept worse. Although I prefer being in your bed."

Willow almost choked on her toast, and Ethan physically jumped as he realized what he had said. He held up a hand, color spreading across his cheeks. "I meant in your spare room, of course. I didn't…" He gave up and closed his eyes with an embarrassed frown.

She giggled and leaned forward to reach for her mug of coffee. "I know what you meant." She watched him over the rim of her coffee, enjoying his discomfort. "It all sounds remarkably quiet outside. Looks like the storm's gone."

He was clearly relieved at the change of subject. "Yes, it's blown over, the power is back on, and hopefully it's going to warm up a little and start to thaw." He pushed himself from the chair with a grimace and walked across to the window, pulling back the curtains and staring through the frosted glass, his thumbs hooked in his jeans pocket. The sun hadn't yet risen, but the velvety black sky gradually grew lighter.

She saw the tension in the set of his shoulders, the angle of his head.

"You need to leave, don't you?" For some reason, the thought left a hollow feeling in the pit of her stomach.

For a moment he didn't acknowledge her words, but then he turned slowly to fix her with that intense gaze. A muscle pulsed in his jaw as he struggled with an internal conversation she didn't understand. "I need to speak to Mike is what I need to do," he said, eventually.

"Mike?"

He sat down in the armchair again, wincing slightly and shifting his position to ease the pull on his stitches. Leaning forward, he rested his elbows on his knees, running a hand through his hair. After a while, he met her gaze. "Yes, I need to leave." He glanced toward the lightening sky. "That is, if it begins to thaw and the road clears enough for me to leave…"

He licked his lips, his eyes shifting from one object in the room to another, clearly mulling something over in his head. "But I'm not sure it's safe."

"You think they'll be looking for you? They'll try to find you?"

He shook his head slowly, lifting his gaze to hers. "Not me," he said, quietly. "You."

"Me?" She blinked and gave a startled laugh. "Why would they be looking for me?"

He blew out a long breath. "You said it yourself the other day. They were close enough to blow out your wing mirror…close enough to read your license plate. They could trace you."

Willow stared at him. "But why would they? I was just some random car you got into. Surely they'll think you either dumped me out of the car or I dropped you off somewhere."

He wasn't convinced and closed his eyes, pinching the bridge of his nose with his finger and thumb. "I need to speak to Mike," he repeated wearily.

"Who's Mike?"

"My handler. My work partner, if you like. The guy I've been checking in with while I've been undercover," he elaborated with a reluctant smile when she raised her eyebrows.

She nodded, waiting for him to expand, but he remained silent. "Do you want to use my phone?"

"Maybe," he said, a frown creasing his brow and indecision darkening his eyes. "I don't know who to trust."

"You don't trust him?"

He immediately shook his head. “It’s not that. But there’s someone on the inside, and that someone will expect me to contact him.”

“Is there someone else you can reach out to?”

She started when he thrust himself from the chair to pace the room. “No one. Someone blew my cover deliberately. It had to be someone on the inside. I’ve spent the last few days trying to figure out who, but I just don’t know. I don’t know who to trust.” He turned. “And I need to make sure you’re safe.”

In a sudden flash of clarity, she understood him, understood what he had been trying to tell her last night. His fear wasn’t for himself, it was for her. She had inadvertently become part of his problem. His fear for her safety was preventing him from acting as he usually would. She knew, without a doubt, that if it wasn’t for her, he would leave as soon as the roads were clear and confront the issue. Knowing his enemies might try and find her made him reluctant to leave.

She moved closer, taking his hands in hers, and waiting until he met her gaze. “You don’t need to worry. Nobody is going to be looking for me.”

Before he could respond, Gwen’s bedroom door opened, and Chappie sprang to life from where he was curled up in front of the fire, giving a delighted bark and running to meet her.

“We can talk about it later.” He ran his thumb along her jaw before stepping away and turning to face Gwen with a warm smile. “Good morning. Right, I’d better get the kettle on.”

Chapter Seven

Willow stared in awe at the jagged tree stump, the huge splinters sharp and evil, evidence of the tremendous force of the storm that had rent the tree so painfully in two. The tree itself lay across the snow-covered playground, its skeletal branches spread out like a fan. Miraculously, the tree had fallen away from the play equipment, and no damage had been done, except to the beautiful old tree itself.

All was calm and still, as if the storm last night had simply been a bad dream, and the sun shone brightly, taking the edge off the chill air. The scent of freshly sawn wood lifted on the slight breeze, and she shivered although even as she looked the snow was melting on the branches of the remaining trees lining the playground. It was beginning to thaw.

A group of men were already surveying the damage when Willow and Ethan arrived, one of them hefting a chainsaw. She recognized Sam's burly figure as he broke away from the group to meet them. "Hi, Sam." She greeted him with a sad frown. "That beautiful, old tree. It's such a shame."

Sam threw a glance over his shoulder. "Aye, but we were lucky it didn't do any more damage." He didn't attempt to hide his curiosity as he looked at Ethan.

She caught his glance. "Oh, sorry. This is Ethan. Ethan, this is Sam."

"I heard you'd got a friend staying with you, Willow." Sam reached out to shake Ethan's hand. "I run The Half Moon across the road. Good to meet you."

"News travels fast." Ethan returned the handshake with a wry smile. "Could you use a hand?" He nodded toward the fallen tree.

"Aye, I reckon we could."

They joined the group gathered around the tree and agreed on a plan of action that would see the tree sawn into logs and distributed around the village for firewood. One of the men hurried off to collect the pile of empty animal feed bags he had piled up in his shed, perfect for carrying the firewood. Ethan eyed the tree and the group of men standing by, ready to pack the logs into the bags.

"Do you know if anyone is checking the village for more storm damage?" he said to no one in particular.

The man holding the chainsaw paused in his attempt to start up the machine. "You've got a point there, friend." He looked around at the group. "Like as not, we don't need all of us for this. How about two of you check around the village?"

"I'll do it," said Willow immediately.

Ethan's gaze narrowed on her, belying his relaxed stance, and when he spoke, his voice was mild. "Are the roads still blocked?"

"No other help is getting through today," said Sam.

She knew it wasn't why Ethan had asked, knew that if the roads had been clear he would have either suggested she stay here or that he would go with her to check the village. As it was, he simply nodded.

"I'll go with you," offered Tom, a slender teenager with a shock of messy, black hair. "This lot will probably get on quicker without me around anyway." He grinned self-consciously and ducked his head when the rest of the men immediately agreed, teasing him with "too right" and "glad you said it, son."

"Come on, Tom." She tucked her arm in his. "They don't want us to see them struggling to lift the logs."

She turned to leave, but a hand on her arm stopped her. She looked up, and her stomach dipped at the familiar, intense gaze.

"I'll see you back at yours later, okay?" Ethan's voice was low, gentle, and it caused a warm glow to spread through her despite the cold air.

"Okay." She frowned a little. "And you need to watch those stitches."

"Don't worry about me." He looked as if he was going to say more; in the end he just nodded.

As she turned away to catch up with Tom, she caught sight of Sam staring after her. She lifted her eyebrows in a question, wondering if he was going to say something, but he dropped his gaze and bent down to pick up a log, his expression unreadable.

****

The cottage was cold when Willow got home. It was mid-afternoon, and she was starving but after a quick deliberation decided she needed warmth before food. She and Tom had made their way around the village, knocking on doors to check if anyone needed any help. They had picked up a few more volunteers along the way too, which was handy as several fences had blown down and were quickly set about by men wielding hammers, nails, saws, and sledgehammers.

She and Tom had helped to clear quite a lot of gardens of debris and made several grocery runs to the shop for some of the more elderly villagers before deciding to call it a day.

With the log burner now crackling merrily, she lit a few Christmas scented candles, turned on the television, and tuned in to her favorite festive songs, humming along while she made herself a toasted cheese and ham sandwich. She was just about to sit down, the sandwich halfway to her mouth, when she noticed a white envelope sitting on the doormat, just inside the front door. She took a bite of the sandwich and stared at the envelope. Had it been there when she came in? Surely, she would have seen it if it had been. But she hadn't heard anyone drop it through the letterbox either.

Swallowing her mouthful, she set her plate down on the coffee table before going to pick up the envelope. Her name was written on the front in small, neat capitals. It felt like a card. She opened the front door curiously, peering up and down the road, but saw no one. A quick glance at the path and the doorstep showed two sets of footprints, one of which was hers. But had the other set been there when she came home? It was entirely possible, she supposed. She had been cold, tired, and hungry and thinking of nothing else but getting home and putting her feet up. Not that it mattered, she shrugged. It was just strange that she hadn't either seen it when she came in or heard someone put it through her door.

Pulling the door shut behind her, Willow sat down in the chair by the fire and tore open the envelope, singing along softly to the song on the television. She smiled at the idyllic scene depicted on the card, children in Victorian costume ice-skating on a frozen village pond while others bought wares from the little stalls surrounding it. Glitter sparkled on the trees, on the tops of the stalls, and on the stars scattered over the midnight blue sky.

Taking another bite of her sandwich, she opened the card, and froze. She stared at the single word scrawled inside.

WHORE!!

Blinking in disbelief, she swallowed hard to get rid of what was now a tasteless, soggy mass in her mouth. She turned the card over, searching for a clue as to who might have sent her such a horrible thing, but there was nothing. Just the usual name of the card company. She opened the card again. Nothing had changed, still the same hateful word written under the printed sentiment "*Have a wonderful Christmas.*"

Willow drew in a long breath as a wave of nausea swept through her. What an awful thing to send. Who on earth would do that? And why? She was well liked in the village, she knew that, and wasn't aware of anyone who might have a grudge against her. She picked up the envelope, but there were no clues, just her name written on the front.

After a moment, she crumpled the envelope in her hand, and threw both it and the card into the log burner. She slammed the door shut, watching the flames burn higher and brighter as the card caught fire, mirroring the sickly burning sensation in the back of her throat.

Sinking back into her chair, she eyed the plate of sandwiches, but her appetite was gone. Instead, she picked up her mug of coffee and cradled it against her chest as she tried to lose herself in the festive tunes but was unable to shake the chill that settled over her like a damp blanket.

****

Willow was struggling to fit the artificial Christmas tree together when she was interrupted by a knock at the door. She paused for a moment, staring at the door as if she could see through it to find out who was standing on her doorstep. There was another knock, and it startled her into action, irritated with herself for her skittishness. Even so, she heaved a sigh of relief when she pulled open the door. “Ethan! It’s you.”

“Were you expecting someone else?” He gave a slight smile. He looked pale and weary, and resisting the urge to throw herself into his arms, Willow stepped back to usher him inside.

“No, but you didn’t have to knock. You should have let yourself in.” She shivered as he moved past her. He smelled of the cold, snow, and ice.

“Can I get you something to eat? You must be starving. I’ll get you something to eat and a hot drink. You’ve been out there for hours. You’re freezing. I can feel how cold you are.” The words tumbled from her mouth as she watched him shrug painfully out of his jacket, wincing in pain, before easing himself into a chair. He held up his hand as if to stem the flow.

“It’s okay. We went back to The Half Moon for something to eat. I could use a hot drink though.” He looked at the plate of sandwiches, sitting forgotten on the table. “Have you only just got in yourself?”

“Oh…no, I’ve been in a while. Just wasn’t hungry.” She disappeared into the kitchen.

Returning five minutes later, she placed the mug of coffee on the table next to him and then turned to resume her struggle with the Christmas tree. Ethan watched her silently for a few seconds and then, with a shake of his head, pushed himself from his chair, and without a word took the tree from her. He slotted the tree into the base before reaching for the top half of the tree and slotting it into the bottom half.

"Thank you." She gave a tight smile but didn't look at him. "I always struggle with that bit." Without looking at him, she began pulling out the branches to spread them evenly, to make it look as realistic as possible. "I usually have a real tree but, well, we're snowed in, and I can't get to the garden center."

"Willow," he said softly. "What's wrong?"

She flashed him a smile and the briefest of glances but didn't pause from arranging the tree. "Nothing's wrong. I'm fine. I just need to get this tree up. I'm late with it this year, and if I don't get it up today, it will be Christmas Eve before I get another chance."

She felt his stare, knew he didn't believe her, but he didn't push and after a moment began helping. "I can't remember the last time I decorated a tree," he said after a while, stepping back to consider where best to place the glittering bauble in his hand.

"Really?" She looked at him in surprise. "Who decorates it then?"

He carefully placed the bauble on one of the topmost branches before giving her a level stare. "I don't usually have a tree. Never really seen the point."

She stared at him as if he were mad. "Not even when you were little?"

"Well, sure we had one when I was younger but not since I left home." He looked at him with a smile, the one that made her stomach dip. "It's not that unusual, is it? Why do you have one? What's the point?"

She reached for another bauble to buy herself some time. Why did she love Christmas so much?

"I don't think there has to be a point, really," she said after a while. "I know some people hate it for its commercialism or because they think it's lost its true meaning. But for me Christmas is a feeling. It's about memories, and tradition, and happiness, and thinking about other people. My Christmas tree is part of that, so are my holiday songs and films." She pointed to the television, still playing her festive music. "And the decorations." She held up the rather crumpled and obviously handmade paper decoration. "One of the children in my class made me this a couple of years ago, and it makes it special, it means something. I don't want my tree to be perfect, all coordinated and soulless, with matching colored baubles. I just…Christmas just makes me happy."

Ethan didn't respond for a moment, simply looked at her with those unreadable gray eyes. Then the corner of his mouth lifted. "I guess I can't argue with that."

****

Willow sank bank into the sofa's soft cushions and closed her eyes contentedly. Ethan was excellent company, although more of a listener than a conversationalist. He was adept at asking thoughtful questions, encouraging her to talk about her childhood, seemingly interested in her reminiscences as they finished decorating the tree and her living room, and then helping her to make a large bowl of chili con carne for supper. She sensed he was deliberately keeping her occupied, as though he knew something had unsettled her, and she wondered at his insight.

She ached to touch him, to draw comfort from him and lean into his strength, but he was deliberately staying just out of reach, just beyond the distance where their hands or arms might inadvertently touch. But his eyes rarely left her, they followed her movements, and she felt his gaze as if he touched her, felt it in the tingle of her skin.

"Well, I'd say you certainly know how to do Christmas." There was a touch of laughter in his voice, and when she opened her eyes she saw him standing in front of her holding out a glass of wine. "I almost feel Christmassy." He gave her the ghost of a wink. "Almost."

She smiled back. "Give me a couple of days, and I'll have you thinking you're Father Christmas himself."

"Probably a good thing the snow is melting then," he responded lightly, once again settling himself in the chair opposite.

She attempted to ignore the sinking feeling in her stomach at his reminder that as soon as the road were clear he would walk out of her life. She forced a light laugh and reached for the television remote to search for a film. "True. Plus, you don't have Father Christmas' twinkly eyes and smile; you'd probably scare the children." She took a mouthful of wine as he gave a soft chuckle.

Ethan's presence had calmed her earlier uneasiness, and she found herself able to dismiss the card as a stupid prank, probably by one of the teenagers in the village. People always talked, and Sam had been quite open about it being well known in the village that she had someone staying with her. Tongues would wag, stirring up gossip to garner a bit of excitement in an otherwise quiet village. Easy then to imagine someone dropping the card through her door as something of a stupid joke, a somewhat misplaced joke, but a joke nonetheless.

What wasn't funny was how much she wanted Ethan to stay, how much she liked it when he leveled that intense gaze at her. She had never met anyone like him before: calm, controlled, and just a little bit dangerous.

"What's bothering you?"

His soft voice broke into her thoughts, and she jumped slightly, spilling a drop of wine over her hand. She saw his eyes darken as he watched her delicately lick the droplets of wine from her skin. Her stomach did a little flip as she saw him take in a breath. "Nothing's bothering me, why?"

"Because we're watching a comedy, one I assume you like seeing as you put it on, and I haven't seen you smile once. And you always smile." His head dropped to one side as he looked at her thoughtfully. "You've been somewhere else all evening."

She didn't answer him directly. "Do you think the roads will be clear tomorrow?"

He gave her an assessing glance, as if trying to work out the reason behind her question. "Jonathan was going to try and get through with the snowplow tomorrow. If it continues to thaw, I reckon he's got a pretty good chance."

He raised his eyebrows when her lips lifted into a small smile.

"You sound like a local." Her smile faded. "And then you'll be leaving."

His expression immediately shifted into an uncharacteristic uncertainty, and he shifted in his seat.

"I don't know. I need to find out what the Hell went wrong but…"

"But you're worried about me," she finished for him. "You're worried that whoever did that to you"—she gestured to his side—"will come looking for me."

The intensity of his gaze, the darkening of his eyes, told her it was exactly what he was thinking. "Look, I told you this morning, I don't think for a second they'll be looking for me."

"That's because you don't live in my world, Willow," he snapped, pushing himself up from the chair and dragging a hand through his hair as he spun away from her. "I feel like I'm in Brigadoon! You live in this…this halcyon world where everybody is so bloody nice and perfect. It's not real; it's a fairytale. It's not my world."

When Willow didn't respond, he took a long breath and flexed his shoulders to ease the tension. He turned around to face her. "I'm sorry. I didn't mean that."

After a moment, she stood and walked over to him, slightly surprised when he didn't retreat from her, and took his hands in hers. She squeezed his fingers gently. "I don't find it so hard to imagine my world is very different to yours." She held his gaze, and then a mischievous grin twitched her lips. "So, in this fairy-tale village, what character do you see me as?"

"You're the beautiful fairy godmother," he said without hesitation. "Granting wishes and making sure everyone is safe and happy."

"And you'd be the mysterious hero, galloping in to rescue the heroine and save the day."

He scowled and would have pulled his hands from hers if she hadn't tightened her grip. "I'm not a hero."

"Well, you make me feel safe."

This time he dragged his hands from hers and once more turned away. "Safe is the last thing I should make you feel."

She stared at his back, saw the tension in the set of his shoulders, and knew she was the cause of his indecision and hesitation. She picked up her wine glass and returned to her seat, tucking her legs beneath her. "Okay, so what do we need to do?"

He turned around slowly to look at her.

"You said this morning that the only person you trust is Mike. So, how do you contact him? I've already said you can use my mobile."

"And I already said they'll be monitoring his calls and emails." He closed his eyes briefly, clearly trying to rein in his irritation.

"Even his personal emails?" She shook her head in frustration. "For Heaven's sake, Ethan, don't you have a…a…safe phone or a code word or something for situations like this?"

"I don't usually expect to be betrayed by someone on the inside; they know all the usual tricks," he snapped, breaking off with a sigh and rubbing the back of his neck. He was silent for a few moments. "Yes, I've got the phone I use to make contact with Mike; but if someone is tracking it, as soon as I switch it on, they'll know where I am. It's too risky."

"Didn't you prepare for something like this?"

Ethan shot her a look of irritation and didn't respond immediately. After a few moments, he sat down opposite her and took a swallow of wine. "Email's not a bad idea."

Despite his ill temper, she continued to offer suggestions. “It’s easy enough to set up a fake account and email Mike. You could get him to ring my mobile on his safe phone or burner phone or whatever it is you call it.”

He continued to mull it over, his gaze never once leaving her face.

“Or,” she said, raising the glass to her lips. “You could just continue doing nothing and stay here with me in fairytale land forever.”

Chapter Eight

"Mike." Ethan pressed Willow's phone to his ear and threw his head back, breathing out a huge sigh of relief. "Christ, it's good to hear your voice."

Willow stood in the doorway between the kitchen and the living room. Ethan had emailed Mike last night, using a newly set up email account and their safe word in the message title. The only message he had sent in the body of the email was her mobile number. But her phone hadn't rung until this morning. She watched Ethan as he looked out of the window. He shook his head.

"No, I'm fine," he said. "I got a bit of a scratch for my trouble, but I'm fine." There was a pause, and then he looked back toward Willow with a smile. "I guess I got lucky. My guardian angel was waiting for me. Just sitting there with the engine idling."

He listened again, frowning. "No, absolutely not. It was pure chance; Willow isn't part of this…no. No chance. I trust her."

She raised her eyebrows. His partner thought she was part of this? She guessed it wasn't so farfetched, could see how it might appear too much of a coincidence.

"Look, Mike, I need to know what the hell's going on. It had to be someone on the inside."

She quietly backed away into the kitchen and closed the door, leaving him to talk to his partner in private. When he eventually came into the kitchen, he found her sitting at the table, surrounded by ribbon, oranges, cloves, and glitter, making more pomanders. She glanced up with a quick smile when he pulled out a chair and sat down. She reached across to turn the volume down on the radio, currently blasting out Christmas carols.

"So, what did Mike have to say?" She continued pressing cloves carefully into her orange, breathing in the spicy, citrus scent it released.

"He's going to do some digging," he said, watching as she finished one pomander and picked up another orange, carefully winding a strip of red ribbon around the middle. "He's like me, struggling to believe we have someone on the inside." He shook his head. "But he agrees it's the only thing that makes any sense."

He picked up an orange and, after glancing across at the one she was working on, began winding the ribbon around it. "He's been keeping the gang under surveillance since he lost contact with me and says it's been pretty quiet; he doesn't get a sense anyone is looking for you. But I can't risk it until we're sure."

Seeing him struggling with the fiddly task, Willow nodded and reached over to help him secure the ribbon to the orange. He flashed her an *"I'm useless"* smile that sent her heart pounding in her chest.

"So, you're not leaving today if Jonathan gets through?" She kept her voice casual, as if it didn't matter either way.

"We've agreed Mike's got twenty-four hours to see if he can find out who is on the inside and confirm no one is looking for you. I'll check in with him tomorrow, and if it's safe I'll go back and speak to the Chief, see if he thinks I've got enough intel to bring Carter in. It's too risky to leave it for much longer.

"Have you got shares in cloves or something?" he carried on after a pause, carefully sticking the cloves into his orange.

She laughed and reached for the next orange. "I should have, shouldn't I?"

They fell into silence, or rather Ethan did as Willow sang along to the carols, enjoying surreptitiously watching him as he concentrated on his task.

"Don't you get fed up of Christmas carols and music?" he asked suddenly, an amused smile lighting his eyes.

She glanced up. "No. Do you?"

He laughed and didn't answer her but sat back to survey his pomander. He glanced toward hers with a rueful smile. "I'm not much good at this, am I? You've done at least three to my one."

"I've had plenty of practice," she said, picking up his pomander and eyeing it critically. "It's not bad for your first try, to be fair. I usually have the children making them ready for the school fete on Sunday, but with the school closed with the snow I've a fair few to get done before then."

He reached for another orange. "Looks like we'd better crack on then."

An hour later, the box of oranges was empty and had been replaced by row upon row of bright and fragrant pomanders. The entire kitchen smelled of Christmas.

Ethan leaned back in his chair and, bringing his hands to his face, breathed in deeply. "You know, I'll never be able to smell oranges or cloves again without thinking of you." Willow looked up in surprise when he carried on. "Christmas too, of course. It will always remind me of you, singing your songs and watching old movies."

Her breath hitched in her throat as they stared at each other, and then he blinked and shook his head. "Hell, listen to me. I'm getting sentimental." He ducked his head, dropping his gaze from hers. "I tell you, it's this place. It's bewitched."

She wondered if he knew just what effect those words had on her, words he'd uttered without thinking. Would he really walk away tomorrow and never look back? Or would he take the chance to see if the feelings they shared might develop into something stronger? She knew he fought them, was careful to control them, but surely at some point he would allow himself to get close to someone?

She looked up to find him observing her keenly, and color warmed her cheeks as if he was able to read her thoughts. "You'd better prepare yourself for full on festivity tonight at The Half Moon party," she said with a wicked grin. "Sam never does anything by half."

****

She sprayed a little glitter gel onto the very tips of her hair and brushed shimmering dusting powder along her collar bones and over her shoulders before standing back to check her appearance in the mirror. The black Gypsy style skirt fell in tiers to her toes, and while the black, Bardot-style top could have made for a somber outfit, the red tasseled belt cinching in her waist and the matching red lipstick and red sparkling drop earrings lent her a festive air. She pulled the top a little farther down her shoulders and turned this way and that to check the effect, pleased with the way the glitter caught the light, before reaching for a dark red comb and using it to secure one side of her hair behind her ear.

Butterflies fluttered in her stomach making her feel jittery; she was nervous, wondering what Ethan would think when he saw her. He'd certainly already seen her at her worst first thing in a morning, so she hoped he liked what he saw now she had made an effort with her appearance. Her eyes shone brightly, filled with anticipation as she looked at her reflection, and she blew out a breath, trying to control her nerves. It was only a party at the local pub, just like many she had been to before.

But not with Ethan, whispered the little voice in her head, *not when it's been this important before.* She gave a shrug as if shrugging off the annoying voice and turned from the mirror to run lightly down the stairs and into the living room, where he was waiting for her.

He turned as she walked in, and his reaction was everything she had hoped for. His gaze took in her twinkling hair and ruby red lips before lingering on the sparkling dust over her collar bones. His eyes darkened before dropping lower to her waist and down to her toes before slowly traveling back up to once more rest on her lips. His chest lifted as he drew in a long breath, and a wolfish expression lifted the corner of his mouth. She felt his hunger for her radiating from him in waves, saw it in the way his fists clenched by his sides as if he was physically restraining himself from reaching for her.

Willow's stomach dipped in response to his reaction; her skin tingled wherever his gaze rested on her as if he had physically touched her as he so obviously wanted to do. He closed his eyes for the briefest moment, and when he opened them again the wolfish expression was gone, and he was once more in control. He moved across the room toward her, stopping just beyond reach as if still not trusting himself.

"You look absolutely stunning." He gave a half smile before his voice dropped to a growl. "And I swear you are doing this on purpose."

She looked at him with an innocent expression. "What do you mean?"

"You know exactly what I mean." The wolf briefly flashed in his eyes before he relaxed into a smile. "And I am completely underdressed."

"Hardly." She allowed her gaze to travel from his head to his toes, ignoring the blush stealing across her cheeks. "You look very handsome. How many outfits do you have stashed in your duffel bag? It must be like Mary Poppins' carpet bag."

"I'm afraid this is it. I've exhausted my wardrobe." Ethan glanced down at the clean black jeans and crisp white shirt that accentuated his taught, slim physique, and her heart thumped in her chest as she remembered the defined muscles hidden beneath the shirt. Perhaps he was able to read her expression because his eyes darkened once more, and he took another step back. "I think we'd better go, don't you?"

His expression lightened when he saw her pulling on black, sparkly wellington boots, and he raised his eyebrows.

Willow looked up at him and suppressed a grin. "You don't think so?"

He shrugged in response, clearly not wanting to offend her.

"Don't worry, I'm taking these to change into." She held up a pair of black, low heeled pumps before slipping them into her shoulder bag.

"Ah. You've clearly done this before."

Chapter Nine

The Half Moon looked cozy and inviting as they walked up the lane. Warm yellow light spilled from the windows, casting a soft glow onto the snow outside, and sounds of conversation and laughter could be heard as they drew nearer. Willow walked in through the storm shelter entrance and then stopped to turn to Ethan, catching her breath when she realized how close he was. His hands gripped her waist to steady her as she rocked backward in surprise.

"Sorry," she said, somewhat breathlessly. "I just wanted to say thank you for coming with me tonight. I know it's probably not really your sort of thing."

His gaze dropped to her ruby red lips, and his fingers tightened slightly around her waist. He really was very close. "My pleasure."

For a moment neither one spoke until someone opened the door to the lounge and the spell was broken. Ethan released her as she turned to the newcomer.

"Willow. I thought I saw you walking up."

Hanging up her coat on the hooks by the door, she bent down to pull off her boots and put them in the corner of the shelter. "No one nick my wellies!" she called to no one in particular through the open door. She slipped on her pumps as shouts of laughter followed her words.

"Ha ha. I can just see Jonathan tramping through the fields in your glittery boots, Willow. You'd better watch out. I bet he's got his eyes on those!" someone shouted from the other side of the room.

Jonathan, standing by the bar, colored a little but took the jesting in good humor.

The pub was already busy, and the noise and the warmth as they walked into the room made her blink. Laughter and loud conversation battled with the usual Christmas songs over the speakers, and Willow scanned the room, smiling when she saw one of her girlfriends waving from a booth at the far end and gesturing that she had saved them a seat. Grabbing Ethan's hand, she made her way across the crowded room and sank gratefully into the seat next to her friend.

"Gosh, I can't believe how busy it is already. Carrie, thank you so much for saving the seat." She gave her friend a kiss and a hug before turning to Ethan. "Ethan, this is my friend, Carrie."

He reached across the table to shake her hand. "Good to meet you."

Carrie's mouth opened and closed a couple of times before she managed a strangled "Hi."

"Ladies, what can I get you to drink?" Ethan gestured to Carrie's half empty glass, and she at last found her voice.

"Oh, no, it's okay, I'm good, thanks."

"I'll have a white wine, please." Willow giggled at her friend's uncharacteristic reticence and turned to her as Ethan made his way to the bar. "What's the matter with you? I've never known you to refuse a drink before."

Carrie joined in her laughter. "Well, firstly can I say, you look absolutely fabulous. And secondly, who is that gorgeous man? You could have warned me. Oh, my God. Just look at him."

They both turned to look at Ethan as he stood by the bar, laughing and joking with some of the men he had been working with at the school yesterday morning. He glanced across and, catching her watching him, gave her a brief wink before turning back to the bar to pay for the drinks.

"I've died and gone to heaven." Carrie sighed and sat back in her seat. "Bless them. The village lads don't stand a chance. Look at them, standing up straight, puffing out their chests. Even my Paul. Ethan's a different breed, and they know it."

Willow knew what she meant, and Ethan's words came back to her. *It's not my world.*

No, it wasn't. But that didn't mean it couldn't be, did it? The men might automatically sense competition, but they clearly didn't resent him and had quickly welcomed him into their group.

Carrie's elbow in her side brought her attention back. "So, come on then. Tell me all about him. Where did you meet him, what does he do?"

"I met him in York, literally just bumped into him, to be honest." Willow smiled at the little white lie. "And, he's a…a detective with the police."

"Ooohh, he can investigate me anytime he wants."

"Carrie."

Her friend gave an unrepentant shrug, her eyes once more drawn to the bar. "That's it though. He's not especially tall, not particularly muscular, but there is definitely something about him. He can take care of himself; you can tell."

Willow nodded. It was that dangerous quality she found so attractive.

"Anyway, shush, he's coming over."

Ethan placed a glass on the table in front of Willow, along with a bottle of wine and a knowing glance at the two women. "Thought it might save fighting through to the bar too often." He set his own pint of beer on the table and glanced back to the bar as the music was turned down and someone tapped a microphone to check it was working.

"Good evening, ladies and gentlemen." Sam did his best compere impression behind the bar. "Now, before we start the evening's festivities, I'd like us to raise a glass to Jonathan for his sterling effort in clearing Lowfield Lane this morning and linking us back into the main road. I know it took some doing, and I understand there were a few hairy moments, but you made it, and I just wanted to say we appreciate it." Sam raised his glass. "Tonight, Jonathan, your drinks are on the house. So, everyone raise a glass to Jonathan."

Everyone in the room chorused "To Jonathan."

"Okay, this is your five-minute warning," Sam continued, clearly beginning to relax into his role. "We're going to be starting our evening's entertainment with a quiz, so get yourselves into your best teams."

As people shuffled around, arranging themselves into teams, Ethan slid into the booth next to Willow, and Carrie beckoned to Paul. Another couple joined them, and as they crammed into the tight space next to Carrie and Paul, Ethan shifted slightly to rest his arm along the back of the bench, creating a little more room as he pulled Willow closer into his side. He had deliberately moved to ensure no one was sitting on his injured side, and she glanced up at him as his fingers brushed her shoulder. There was a flurry of introductions, and then the quiz started and the room fell into an expectant hush.

Half an hour later, the winning team was announced and the noise levels in the room had resumed their former level. Paul complained good naturedly that their team had been at a disadvantage because Carrie and Willow had not taken the quiz seriously enough and had been too busy talking to listen to the questions. It was clear as the evening progressed that their table wasn't going to win any of the games, but it didn't matter; Willow was unable to concentrate on anything other than the delicious sensations Ethan's fingers caused as they continued to draw lazy circles along her shoulders, brushing her collar bone and the nape of her neck. Sitting so close, unable to keep his usual distance, he appeared unable to stop himself from touching her, and she took full advantage, resting her hand lightly on his thigh.

He leaned close to whisper in her ear. "Is Sam the ex you were talking about the other day?"

His breath tickled her neck causing a tingling sensation to shiver down her spine, and she turned to look up at him in surprise. "Why do you say that?"

He smiled slowly and gave the bar the slightest nod of his head. "Because he's not been able to stop looking over at our table all evening."

Automatically turning to glance across at Sam, she gasped when Ethan caught her chin with his finger and slowly leaned into her. "Don't, he's looking over at us."

As he held her gaze, Willow's breath caught in her throat, and the sounds of the pub faded into the distance when he dipped his head the fraction needed to kiss her, a gentle, lingering kiss that was everything she had craved all evening.

A crash sounded, breaking into their little bubble, with Ethan pulling away as cheers sounded around the bar, and several people jokingly accused Sam of having butter fingers. Looking across at Sam, she saw his ruddy cheeks glowing with even more color than usual. He shrugged the comments off with a good-natured grin as he bent to sweep up the broken glass, having obviously dropped a bottle of something or other.

"Yeah, yeah, it's easy done." He waved a hand at the men heckling him. "Trying to do too many things at once, as usual. Rubbish at multitasking is what it is."

She turned back to Ethan, who had raised an eyebrow, but she frowned and shook her head. "You're imagining things. Yes, he's my ex, but it's all done and dusted. We're just friends, and that's how we like it."

She could see he wasn't convinced, but she knew Sam, and she knew herself. There was nothing there anymore, hadn't really been anything serious to begin with, if she was being honest with herself.

****

It was late in the evening, and Willow was feeling slightly lightheaded from the wine and from Ethan's nearness. She noticed he had deliberately not kept pace with the others at the table in terms of alcohol intake and knew he was keeping a clear head. She had followed suit, although she had drunk more than he had, and now, as they were standing by their table, was grateful for his arm around her waist as she leaned into him. It was a merry atmosphere, and her cheeks ached from laughing so much.

They had just finished a ridiculous game where everyone in the room had arranged themselves into two, more or less straight lines and then had to pass an orange from one person to the other without using their hands. It had taken several minutes for each line to complete the task, not helped by copious amounts of alcohol having been consumed throughout the night, and people bent double with laughter.

"Okay, let's have a five-minute breather," said Sam over the microphone. He turned the music up a little, and as a slow ballad filtered through the room several couples began to dance.

Ethan's hand tightened on her waist, and Willow looked up as he took her hand and pulled her close, swaying in time to the music. Her stomach quivered as she slipped her hands over his shoulders, her cheek resting against his. She was certain he must be able to feel her heart thumping in her chest and closed her eyes when his hand splayed across the small of her back, pulling her even closer so their hips brushed against each other as they moved. His other hand teased her hair, and as she lifted her head he brushed her cheek with his fingers, the look in his eyes filling her with heat and desire. The corner of his mouth lifted slightly, and he gave the slightest shake of his head, as if having an internal conversation with himself, but when he lowered his head, instead of kissing her it was to allow her to lean her head against his shoulder.

Swallowing her disappointment, Willow once more closed her eyes as they danced, losing herself in the moment, savoring the sensation of his body against hers, the feel of his muscles flexing beneath her fingers as they moved. She smiled against his shoulder, slipping her fingers into the hair at the nape of his neck, and was rewarded when his arms tightened and he dropped a kiss on her bare shoulder. In this moment, this was everything she could ever need or want.

They had been dancing for several minutes when a wave of uneasiness swept through her, and she opened her eyes with a snap. The atmosphere was suddenly heavy, weighted with expectation. She glanced around the room uneasily. Her gaze stopped on the figure of a man standing in the doorway across the room.

And was immediately rocked by a wave of negative energy.

He was a tall, broad shouldered man, but she could see little else beneath the black hooded sweatshirt he wore, the hood pulled so low that his face was in shadow. Dark negativity radiated from him, and she blinked as a stab of pain lanced through her head. Ethan clearly sensed her discomfort because he pulled away, his fingers still resting on her waist.

"Hey, you okay?"

She dragged her gaze from the figure in the doorway to Ethan and then across to the bar to see if Sam was aware of the stranger, but he wasn't there. No one else in the pub appeared to have noticed the man or, if they had, saw nothing amiss.

Ethan's fingers tightened when she didn't respond. "Willow?"

"That man in the doorway…" Her voice trailed off.

The doorway was empty.

Ethan turned to follow her gaze, frowning when he too saw it was empty. He looked around the room, as if searching for whoever might have caused her discomfort. “Who? What man?”

The dark figure was nowhere to be seen. The atmosphere had returned to its former light merriment, and the pain in her head had receded. She knew without a doubt the man was no longer there.

“He’s gone.”

“Who was it? What did he look like?”

They were standing in the middle of the room with other couples still dancing around them oblivious to anything amiss, and after a quick glance at her face Ethan led her back to their table. He slipped his arm around her shoulder so they could talk quietly.

“What is it?”

Willow shrugged uncertainly, not sure how to explain just why the man had affected her so. “I don’t know. It was just odd. He was standing in the doorway, staring at us.”

He nodded slowly, his eyes never once wavering from her face. “What did he look like?”

“I’m not sure. He was all in black. He was tall, broad, and was wearing a black hoodie, pulled forward so I didn’t see his face.”

Ethan stared at her in silence.

“There was just something about him. It felt all wrong.” She looked at him unhappily, seeking reassurance. “He was just staring at us.”

He nodded again. “Are you sure he was looking at us? You said you didn’t see his face.” His voice was carefully neutral.

Aware of how paranoid she sounded, she pulled away, but Ethan’s hand tightened on her shoulder.

"Hey, I believe you. I'm just trying to understand why it upset you so."

"I don't know. And you're right, I couldn't see his face…but I know it was us he was looking at." She dropped her gaze to her hands, fiddling with the tassels on her belt. "Don't ask me how I know, I just do."

He hooked a finger under her chin, gently lifting her face toward him. "Want me to have a look around?"

Willow shook her head immediately. "No, no, it's fine. Look, he's gone. I'm sorry, I don't know why I'm making such a fuss; it's no big deal. He clearly didn't bother anyone else. I don't know what it was about him, but…there was just something not right."

The more she tried to explain, the more her uneasiness faded, until she was less certain about how the man had affected her. She was overreacting. "I'm fine. I guess I was just surprised because we don't usually get strangers here. It was just a bit of a shock, that's all."

She smiled up at Ethan, snuggling in against him as his fingers once more swirled those gentle circles over her shoulder, soothing her discomfort. "I don't want you to go anywhere; I like you just where you are."

She lifted her face to his, knew from the hunger in his eyes that he wouldn't be able to resist, and as he dropped his head to catch her lips with his all thoughts of the stranger were forgotten.

Far too soon, Sam's voice broke in over the microphone, gathering everyone back to the festivities and allowing Ethan to break their kiss, his expression clearly telling her he knew just how easily he had fallen into her trap. Fizzing with happiness, Willow was once more soon swept up in party games and laughter.

****

"Oh, don't you wish you could stay here in Brigadoon?" Willow stumbled in the snow and clung onto Ethan as he steadied her against him, laughter rumbling deep in his chest. "I think I'm a little drunk," she giggled, covering her mouth with her hand.

"I think I'd agree." He grasped her shoulders and gently turned her away from him, pushing her toward the way they were headed. The party had ended just after midnight, and now they made their way back to her cottage. It was a beautifully clear night, and the stars crowded the sky without a single cloud to obscure them. The moon shone brightly, and their breath created complicated swirls in the in the chill night air.

"I can't believe you've actually watched Brigadoon," she carried on, not seeming to mind that he hadn't answered her question. "You said you never watched films."

Ethan tucked her arm in his. "I don't usually, but I have seen that one. Years and years ago. It's one of my mum's favorites, actually."

"And did you like it?" She gripped his arm a little tighter as one foot slipped in the snow. For some reason she was finding it more difficult to walk than usual.

"It was an interesting concept."

She arranged her face into a mock-serious expression. "It was an interesting concept," she repeated, with an attempt at a stuffy, upper class accent. "It was a fabulous, mystical, and deeply romantic film, is what I think you're trying to say."

His mouth turned up into a grudging smile as she stopped and tried to focus her gaze on him. "Okay, yes, I'm sure that's what I was trying to say." He steered her through the gate to her cottage. "Right, we're here. Where are your keys?"

Willow rummaged through her shoulder bag and handed him the keys, turning away as he walked down the path to her front door. It really was so clear, the moon shining so brightly there was no need for the streetlights. She glanced down the road toward the village and drew in a sharp breath. She sobered up in an instant.

Standing a little way down the road, facing toward her, was the man in the hoodie. He was standing beneath a streetlight, his face in shadow. Once again, a stab of pain lanced through her head.

"Ethan," she managed in a strangled voice. She reached behind her, but he was too far away.

He was struggling to turn the key. "This bloody lock is stiff."

"Ethan!" This time her voice was louder.

She hurried down the path, reluctantly turning away from the figure. She grasped Ethan's arm.

"I'm trying." He was laughing, but when she shook his arm and pulled him away from the door, he realized something was wrong. "What? What is it?"

"He's there." Her breath was coming in short, sharp gasps as she pointed down the road. "The man from the pub. He's there again."

Ethan stared at her for a moment before pushing past her to stride to the gate. He looked along the road they had just walked. "Where? I can't see him."

"He's there. Under the lamp post." She broke off as she drew up at the gate beside him and saw the road was empty. The man had disappeared. "Oh, Ethan, he was there. I promise he was; he was just standing there." She ended on a sob, shaking her head in confusion, knowing he wasn't going to believe her.

But instead of arguing, he gripped her hand and pulled her back to the door, this time turning the key in the lock first time. He gently pushed her inside and handed her the key. "Get in, lock the door behind me, and don't open it for anyone except me, do you hear?"

"What are you going to do?" Her voice wavered as she twisted the key in her hands.

"I'm going to see what I can find." His voice was grim and serious.

"Oh, please don't, Ethan." She caught hold of his sleeve and pulled him into the cottage. "Please don't. He doesn't feel safe. He feels…he feels evil."

He loosened her fingers from his arm and ducked his head to look at her. "Nothing is going to happen to me. I'm just going to have a look around."

He stepped back onto the path. "Lock the door, and don't open it until I get back, okay? I mean it."

Willow nodded reluctantly, and when he didn't move, clearly waiting to make sure she locked the door, she closed it quietly before turning the key in the lock.

She leaned her forehead on the door for a few seconds, taking long, deep breaths in an effort to steady her breathing. Hot chocolate. She could make some hot chocolate to keep herself busy until Ethan got back. She nodded to herself; yes, that was a good idea.

Reaching for the light switch, she winced as light flooded the room and squinted as her eyes adjusted to the change and then blinked in confusion. Her gaze focused on the white envelopes scattered haphazardly over the carpet.

The room appeared to lurch beneath her feet, and she flung out a hand to steady herself against the wall as her knees threatened to give way. Swallowing hard, she slowly reached for the nearest card, the one she was standing on, and picked it up, her fingers gripping the envelope tightly. Her hand was shaking so much she could hardly read her name, written in those familiar, small, neat capitals. A sob escaped her lips.

Chapter Ten

Willow placed the pile of envelopes on the coffee table, nibbling on the edge of one of her nails and squeezing her eyes shut against the tears threatening to fall. After a moment, she turned and ran up the stairs to the spare room and across to the window to peer along the street. The road was deserted. There was the lamp post where the stranger had been standing, but neither he nor Ethan were anywhere to be seen.

Everything was quiet and peaceful, completely at odds with the fear spiking through her chest. "Come on, Ethan. Where are you?"

She stood so close to the window her breath misted the glass. She remained there, moving from one foot to the other, suffused with nervous energy. After a couple of minutes, she turned and went downstairs.

Those hateful envelopes still sat where she had left them. She eyed them warily, as if expecting them to suddenly spring up from the table and whirl like angry bees. Fear turned to anger. How dare someone try to frighten her? Why else thrust so many cards through her door? A single card yesterday was one thing. This was something else.

She strode to the table and snatched an envelope from the top of the pile, tearing it open. Barely glancing at the sparkling, snow covered scene on the front, similar to the card yesterday, she opened it and read the single word inside.

SLUT!!

She stared at it for a few long seconds, breathing through her nose before tossing it onto the table and reaching for the next card.

TRAMP!!

Willow systematically worked her way through all the envelopes, twenty-five in total, all containing a single word, all variations on a theme. By the time she had opened all the envelopes, her anger had receded and her stomach once again rolled with fear, her fingers trembling so much toward the end that she was barely able to open the last envelope.

The controlled, almost measured way the cards had been written, printed in careful, neat capital letters, was more frightening than the words themselves. The aim of the sender was deliberate and dedicated. It wasn't just someone sending through a card in a fit of pique or as a teenage prank.

A loud thumping on the front door had Willow springing to her feet, a cry of alarm escaping her lips.

"Willow, it's me." Ethan's voice was muffled through the wood.

She flew to unlock the door, flinging it open to find him thumping his boots against the step. He stepped over the threshold, locked the door, and turned around just in time to catch her as she flung herself into his arms, burying her face against his shoulder.

"Hey, hey. It's okay." Taken by surprise, he hesitated a split second before wrapping his arms around her. He leaned back a little to look at her, but she clung to him, and he allowed her to stay in his embrace. “Hey, you’re shaking. What is it? Did something happen?”

“Willow.” His voice sharpened when she didn’t respond. “Did something happen?”

She reluctantly stepped back from him. “Yes, I mean no, not really. I don’t know. I’m sorry.” As he took her hand and pulled her to sit next to him on the sofa, she gestured at the cards scattered across the coffee table. “These were pushed through the letterbox.”

Ethan frowned and reached for the nearest card, pausing briefly to look at the front before opening it. He stiffened when he read the word inside, flicking her a swift, searching glance before picking up the next card, and the next, until he had read them all.

She sensed the anger radiating from him, although outwardly he remained calm. The only visible evidence of his anger was the pulse throbbing steadily in his jaw.

“These were put through the door this evening?” His voice was quiet and even. “You haven’t had any before? Anything like this?”

“I received one yesterday. When I got back at lunchtime.”

His lips tightened as he took this information in, and she saw him understand the reason for her unease yesterday.

“Do you think it’s them?” Her voice wavered as she asked the question that had been preying on her mind since she had first seen the stranger earlier. “Do you think it’s Carter’s gang? Was that who was following us tonight?”

He didn’t answer immediately and instead got up and walked through to the kitchen. Unsure what to do, Willow began carefully gathering the cards together, stacking them neatly into a pile on the table. When he returned, he was carrying two mugs of hot chocolate, and he handed one to her with a slight smile.

"Here. There's a nip of brandy in there too."

He turned sideways to face her on the sofa. "I didn't see anything or anyone out there…"

"I'm not making it up—"

He held up his hand. "I'm not saying you are. I'm saying I didn't see anything. Whoever it was you saw was long gone."

He blew out a breath and ran a weary hand over his face. "And I'm not sure the two are linked." He picked up one of the cards and shook his head. "These? These are definitely not Carter. It's not his style. He's not into playing games. And that's what this is. Someone is playing, trying to frighten and intimidate you."

"Well, they're succeeding." She managed a wan smile, blowing across the mug before taking a tentative sip and eying him uncertainly above the rim. "What about whoever was following us? You do believe me, don't you? About the guy in the hoodie?"

Her heart skipped a beat when he shook his head.

"One thing at a time." He waved the card. "Can you think of anyone in the village who might do this? I think it's obvious my being here has prompted it."

"No. There isn't anyone who would do something like this. It's just horrible. No one in the village is that cruel, that hateful."

"No one?" Ethan continued to probe, his voice carefully neutral. "You can't think of anyone who might be unhappy with me being here?"

Willow slammed her mug down on the table and pushed up from the sofa to stare at him angrily. "I know what you're getting at. You think Sam did this because…because you think he's jealous or something. But you're wrong. He would never do something like this. Never."

"Are you sure?"

"Yes, I'm sure." Aware her voice was rising, she took a deep, calming breath. "Sam couldn't have done this anyway. He was at the pub all night with us, you know that."

He leaned back against the sofa. "There was at least one point this evening when Sam wasn't there. It would only take five minutes, ten at the most, to run up here, push the cards through, and get back to the pub without anyone really noticing."

"God, you're so suspicious of everyone." She thrust her hands through her hair in agitation. "Is this what it's like for you? Always thinking the worst of people?"

"What, you mean just like you always think everyone is sweetness and light? You're too bloody trusting."

"No. No, I'm not. I'm just normal." She was positively shaking with anger now, unable to believe that Sam could be behind something so awful. "And I'm not going to stand here and listen to you accuse my friend. Sam didn't do this. So you can take your nasty little suspicions and think of someone else."

When Ethan simply stared at her, she spun away from him before turning to run upstairs to her room and slamming the door behind her.

****

Ethan closed his eyes and blew out a long breath, leaning forward to rest his elbows on his knees, head in his hands. This was what he had been afraid of; the road was clear, and within hours they were possibly being stalked by Carter's gang.

But something niggled, something wasn't right; it just didn't feel like Carter.

He knew without a doubt that Willow was telling the truth, even though he hadn't seen the hooded stranger himself. He equally had no doubt that Sam had sent the cards. He was a jealous bastard, but not dangerous; Ethan wasn't worried about him.

He pushed himself from the sofa and walked over to the window, pulling aside the curtains to stare out at the moonlit view. All was calm and peaceful, with no sign of any intruder. Cold air radiated from the glass, and he shivered, dropping the curtains and stepping back from the window.

Moving across to the front door, he locked and bolted it before going through to the kitchen. He unlocked and opened the back door, stepping out onto the path to look around, his gaze searching for anything amiss, any sign that the stranger was or had been near the cottage. Again, all was still; there was only a single set of footprints on the path that he knew belonged to Willow. With a final glance around, he stepped back into the kitchen and locked the door before pulling the kitchen blinds shut.

Satisfied the cottage was secure, he slowly walked back into the living room to stand in front of the log burner. He pulled Willow's phone from his pocket and stared at it, chewing his lip in uncharacteristic indecision. Cursing under his breath, he tapped in Mike's number and held the phone to his ear.

Mike answered on the second ring. "Ethan, you okay?"

"Sorry to call so late. I'm fine, but things are kicking off here." When he got no response, he pushed. "What's happening your end? Any movement with Carter's gang?"

"Nope, quiet as a mouse over here. Why, what's happened?"

"Are you sure? You haven't seen any movement, anything unusual?"

"No, nothing." Mike's voice buzzed in his ear. "Carter's carrying on as usual, no drama, no change. Ethan, what's going on?"

"I don't know. Someone's hanging around. When I spoke to you this morning, I said we were hoping the road was going to be cleared. Well, it's clear, and now someone's hanging around. I don't like it."

"You think it's Carter?"

Ethan hesitated. "I don't know. It doesn't feel like him, but I don't know. I don't know who else would be following us."

"What does he look like?"

Again, Ethan hesitated. "I haven't gotten a look at him, but Willow's seen him twice. Tall, broad, and wearing a black hoodie, with the hood pulled low over his face."

There was a pause. "You haven't seen him yourself?"

"No. Willow saw him at the pub while we were there tonight and then again when we were walking home. He was following us."

"But you didn't see him?"

"No, I didn't see him."

There was an even longer pause. "Are you sure there was someone there?"

"Yes, I am." Ethan strove to keep his tone even. "What, you think she was lying or seeing things?"

"I don't know, you tell me." Mike sighed down the phone. "Look, what do you even know about this girl, Ethan?"

"I know I trust her."

When his partner didn't respond, Ethan closed his eyes, halfway between wanting to scream and wanting to weep. "Mike, please…"

"Okay," he said eventually. "Look, we're buddies, I'm your partner. Of course, I'm going to help you. You say the road is clear, so I'll come through first thing in the morning, and we can check this thing out."

Ethan's knees nearly buckled with relief. "Thanks."

"But hey, just…just think about it, okay?" Mike persisted.

"I'll see you in the morning."

He ended the call, resisting the urge to throw the phone across the room. God, he was tired, and the stabbing pain in his side told him he had done far too much physical activity over the last couple of days. He needed to get some rest, to make sure he was ready for whatever the next few days were going to bring.

Switching off the light, he made his way slowly up to the spare room. He paused outside Willow's bedroom door, wishing she hadn't been so angry with him. It worried him that she was so trusting, so determined to see the good in everyone. A frisson of desire sparked through him as he thought of the kisses they had shared tonight, of the feel of her skin beneath his fingers as he caressed her shoulders, and the soft line of her collar bone. He had never met anyone who made him feel so out of control, and he didn't like that feeling.

He turned away from her door abruptly. He had allowed himself to get too close tonight; it blurred his focus, his instincts, just when he needed them most. It was no good, he had to keep his distance.

****

Willow awoke the next morning with a splitting headache, having slept fitfully all night, unable to stem the thoughts swirling around her head. She refused to believe Sam was behind the horrible cards, no matter how much she trusted Ethan. He was just too used to dealing with the wrong sort of people and saw lies and mistrust everywhere. It wasn't his fault; she didn't blame him. But if it wasn't Sam, who was it? And why?

She turned over and buried her face in the pillow. It had been such a perfect evening, and it had been ruined, her happiness quickly turning into fear and confusion. She wasn't sure Ethan believed her about the stranger in the hoodie. She had heard the rumble of his voice downstairs after she had gone to bed and wondered who he was talking to. It could only be his partner, Mike; but what had he been saying to him?

Her heart sank when she considered he might have decided she was making it all up. If that was the case, there was no reason for him to stay. Perhaps he had been arranging with Mike to leave today.

Rolling onto her side, she pressed the heels of her hands against her eyes. She couldn't bear the thought of him leaving. What was happening? This wasn't her life; she wasn't the kind of person to have people stalking or following her.

She slowly lifted her hands from her eyes as a new thought occurred to her. Was she certain the stranger had been following her? After all, she had had quite a bit to drink. What if it had just been someone from the party walking home or taking some air?

She sighed; it was so confusing. How could she be sure what she had seen? Did Ethan believe her? Was he even talking to her? She hadn't acted particularly adult last night, running out of the room and slamming the door like a sulky teenager.

She lay back against the pillows, listening to the sounds of him moving around downstairs. It was a comforting sound, one that gave her a warm feeling inside, a feeling of being cared for. She snapped her eyes open.

Where had that come from?

She loved her life, loved living alone in her cozy little cottage. She had never been lonely here in the village, so how come the thought of Ethan leaving left her with an aching sense of dread, with a feeling of emptiness?

Annoyed with herself, Willow threw back the duvet and padded into the bathroom to shower, determined to wash away her unsettling thoughts. As always, the view from her bedroom window when she opened the curtains lifted her mood, but the bright sunlight flooding through the window made her wince; she needed something for this wicked headache.

Ethan was in the kitchen when she trudged through in her fluffy slippers, wincing once more at the bright, sunny kitchen.

"Good morning." He smiled, putting a plate of toast and a mug of coffee on the table in front of her as she pulled up a chair. His gaze drew across her pale face. "You okay?"

"It's just a headache." She quickly swallowed the pills she had taken from the bathroom cabinet. "I didn't sleep very well. How about you?"

"I slept okay, thank you." He sat down at the table but made no effort to engage her in conversation. She couldn't blame him.

"I'm sorry about storming off last night," she said eventually. "I just…I just know you're wrong. Sam isn't behind this."

Ethan nodded but made no comment.

"And I know you didn't want to talk about it last night, about whoever it was I saw, but I did see him. And there was something…not right about him."

Again, he made no comment, just fixed her with his usual intense stare.

"Ethan!" Fear that he didn't believe her surged through her, and she clasped her hands together, fingers pressing against her mouth to prevent the plea bursting from her lips. Why wouldn't he speak?

"What do you want me to say?"

She pushed herself away from the table, the chair legs scraping noisily across the floor. "I want you to say you believe me."

He looked at her. "I do believe you."

"I…you do?"

He responded with a half-smile. "Yes, I do."

"Oh." She returned to her seat, cheeks burning with the realization she had probably over-reacted…again. She picked up her toast and took a bite, her gaze firmly fixed on her mug of coffee. "But you didn't see anyone when you went out to look last night."

"That doesn't mean I don't believe you saw someone."

There was a long pause as she finished her toast. Ethan didn't seem particularly inclined to break the silence.

"What do you think? Do you think it was just someone from the village? Some random person?" She looked up uncertainly, her stomach lurching when she realized those gray eyes were already watching her. "Or…or someone from Carter's gang?"

He leaned back in his chair. "I don't know. Look, I spoke to Mike last night, and he's going to come down, help us work through this."

"He's coming here? When?"

Ethan glanced at the clock; it was just before nine a.m. "I imagine any time now. He said he'd be here first thing."

She asked the question to which she dreaded the answer. "Is he going to take you back to York?"

"Not immediately, no." He frowned, rubbing the back of his neck. "Not until we're sure…"

Not until he was sure she was safe. He didn't need to say it. She curled her fingers around her mug of coffee as the silence between them lengthened once more. A sudden thumping on the front door made her jump, and she leapt to her feet, hissing as hot coffee spilled over her fingers. She turned to Ethan with wide eyes.

"It's okay. It'll be Mike."

He got up from his chair and, picking up a tea towel from the work surface, moved toward her and caught her hand. It was the first time he had touched her since last night, and she blinked at the tingling sensation his touch produced, and which she never got used to. He gently dried her hand with the towel before examining her fingers and glancing up at her. "Does it hurt?"

His nearness, his touch, his gentle concern left her speechless, and she simply shook her head. A further knock at the door made them both jump, and Ethan gave a slight smile before dropping her hand.

She followed him from the kitchen but stopped in the doorway to the living room as he carried on through to unlock and pull open the front door.

"Mike."

Chapter Eleven

Ethan opened the door and blew out the breath he hadn't realized he had been holding. Mike Stott stood on the doorstep, shoulders hunched against the cold in a black reefer jacket, black woolen hat, and blue jeans.

"Thank Christ for that, thought I'd got the wrong house there for a minute." He stepped forward over the threshold and shook Ethan's hand, grasping his arm with his other hand.

"Mike. It's good to see you."

He ushered Mike in and closed the door, turning to beckon to Willow. She was leaning against the kitchen door jamb, arms wrapped around herself. She smiled as their eyes met and gave a slight nod, walking into the living room with her hand outstretched toward Mike.

"Mike, this is Willow," said Ethan. "Willow, my partner, Mike."

"It's good to meet you."

She blinked as Mike's hand enclosed hers, and her bright smile faltered. Ethan saw her take in a quick breath and cast a fleeting glance toward him, a glance that made his heart miss a beat. Before he was able to process what that swift glance meant, she was once again smiling up at Mike.

"Gosh, you're cold! Come in and get yourself warm by the fire." She stepped away from him and gestured toward the sofa. "Can I get you a tea, or a coffee?"

"Tea is great, thanks." Mike shrugged out of his jacket, pulled off his hat, and handed them to her with a grateful smile before settling down on the sofa.

Ethan stared after her as she disappeared into the kitchen. What had just happened? Had he imagined her swift glance as she shook Mike's hand? A glance that, to him, had appeared to be full of unease, perhaps even fear. He frowned; she was singing to herself in the kitchen, a familiar sound that always made him smile. He was letting his imagination run away with him; she was probably just reacting to Mike's cold hands, as she had suggested. Mike's voice broke into his troubled thoughts.

"You weren't wrong when you said you were staying in the middle of nowhere." His partner shook his head. "People here in the village might class that road as being open, but let me tell you, it was a white-knuckle ride down here. I'm not sure even your backside is worth that much to Carter's crew."

Ethan grinned, his partner's presence easing some of his tension. "Well, let's hope you're right about that."

He looked up as Willow came through with a tray bearing three mugs and a plate of biscuits, which she placed on the little table in front of the sofa. He saw Mike's gaze taking in the long, black curls, the soft curves not quite hidden beneath the oversized jumper and floor length skirt. He drew in a breath, not liking his partner's assessing gaze. His tension eased when he saw the corner of Mike's mouth lift when he noticed the fluffy slippers peeping from beneath her skirt.

"So, we have you to thank for Ethan being alive today," said Mike, as Willow curled up in the chair opposite, tucking those slippers under her.

She frowned, sipping her coffee. “I think that’s a little over the top; I’m not sure I saved his life.”

Mike raised an eyebrow but obviously decided to let it go. “So, tell me, how come you were there in the first place? From what Ethan’s told me, you were just sitting in your car in the middle of an industrial estate late at night. Fairly unusual, I would say.”

She smiled, her head on one side. “Am I under investigation now?”

Mike gave a short laugh and held his hand up. “Force of habit. Look, I’m just interested, trying to get up to speed with what happened to my partner here.”

“Well, I’m afraid there’s no mystery to it. It’s just that I have a terrible sense of direction. I’d dropped my friend’s son off at the train station, took a wrong turn as I was leaving, and got myself completely lost. I pulled off the road and was putting the satnav on my phone when Ethan…jumped into my car.”

“Bit of a coincidence, don’t you think?”

Willow frowned. “I guess so, but you know, coincidences do happen.”

“Do they?”

It was her turn to laugh. “Yes, of course they do. Sometimes weird things happen; it doesn’t always have to be some premeditated, carefully planned action. It happens quite a lot; it’s why there is a word for it.”

“Maybe.” Mike took another drink of tea. “Okay, let’s say it was a coincidence. But then, what happens next is too much. Then you bring a complete stranger back to your home, a stranger who held you at gunpoint? I find that pretty hard to understand.”

“You sound like Ethan.” She smiled across at Ethan, who was sitting quietly listening. “And for my part, I find it equally hard to believe neither of you would do the same."

"You're not really that naïve, surely?"

There was a long pause. Ethan sensed Willow was wary of his partner, couldn't really blame her. He also saw Mike struggling to believe anyone would do what she had done without an ulterior motive.

"Once you get to know her, you'll realize Willow acted entirely in character," said Ethan quietly.

Mike opened his mouth to respond but shut it without speaking.

Willow changed the subject. "So, what's your plan?"

"Have a scout around, ask a few questions in the village. If someone is hanging around, he can't have gone completely unnoticed." His glance offered a challenge. "I don't care what you say, in a small, close-knit community like this, if no one else saw a stranger hanging around and you were the only one who did, well, that's just too much of a coincidence to stomach."

"You don't believe me." She lifted her chin.

"I don't have any feelings one way or the other at the moment." Mike stood up from the sofa. "That's what we're here to find out."

Both Ethan and Willow got to their feet, and Mike turned to his partner. "You ready?"

"Let's do it." Ethan saw Willow nibble at her lip, a sure sign she was uneasy. "What is it?"

She shrugged, casting a worried glance between the two men. "Just…be careful. He felt dangerous."

"I'm always careful." Mike reached around his back and pulled a gun from the waistband of his jeans. Despite his challenging questions, it was clear he was taking the potential threat seriously. The road was open, it was entirely possible Carter's gang were close, and they couldn't take any chances. He turned to Ethan. "Are you armed?"

"Christ, I can't believe I forgot…" He closed his eyes briefly, furious with his lack of attention. "Willow, what did you do with the firearm? The gun?"

She swallowed and dropped her gaze, turning away to put her mug on the coffee table. "I got rid of it."

There was a beat as both men stared at her.

"You did what?" they said in unison.

"I got rid of it." She met Ethan's gaze defiantly. "I threw it in a ditch somewhere that first morning when I walked down to Gwen's. It'll be buried underneath several inches of snow by now."

Ethan turned from her, his hands clenched into fists at his side, trying to control his frustration. He reminded himself she was a civilian; she didn't understand how it all worked. "Willow. Please tell me you didn't do that." His voice was carefully controlled. "I disarmed one of Carter's men. I have to hand the gun in as evidence."

"It's in the ditch," she repeated, not quite able to hide the tremor in her voice. "I hate guns, especially when they've been pressed against my throat." She deliberately ran her fingers across her arm, across the fading bruises Ethan knew were hidden beneath her jumper. "I might have brought you into my home, but I'm not a complete idiot. I didn't want to risk a gun in the house if you weren't who I thought you were."

He didn't respond, silenced once more by the thought of the bruises he had inflicted.

"Look, we'll deal with that back at the station," Mike said impatiently, casting a disgusted glance toward Willow. “Let’s just get this over with.” He pushed the gun back into the waistband of his jeans and looked expectantly at Ethan. “Come on, let’s go.”

At his words, Willow turned away and went into the kitchen, but not before Ethan saw her stricken expression. “Give me a minute,” he said to Mike.

He followed her into the kitchen, pausing in the doorway. She stood at the sink, staring through the window, her back to him. He moved across and after a slight pause reached out to gently turn her to face him. He hooked a finger under her chin, but she kept her eyes downcast, refusing to meet his gaze.

“Willow, please,” he said when she shook her head. When she eventually lifted her eyes to his, they sparkled with tears, and it was like a punch to his stomach. “What is it?”

“Why does he need the gun? It just makes things worse.”

“It’s just a precaution,” he said with a frown. It hammered home that she really didn’t belong in his world. “But we need to be prepared. You’ve seen what Carter’s gang are capable of. They don’t play games, and we can’t be caught off guard. This is my job. It’s what I do.”

He wrapped her into his arms and held her to him, breathing in the faint traces of her perfume.

“Clock’s ticking, Ethan,” Mike called from the other room.

Ethan’s arms tightened around Willow for a split second before releasing her. He held her away from him and gave her an encouraging smile. Only when she returned his smile did he release her and walk back into the living room, picking up Mike’s jacket and hat on the way through. He tossed them to his partner before picking up Patrick's coat and shrugging into it.

As Mike walked out into the cold morning air, Ethan paused in the doorway. "Lock the door behind us and don't open it for anyone," he told her. "And I mean anyone."

With a sense of déjà vu, he watched as she nodded and closed the door, only turning away when he heard the key in the lock.

****

Willow ran upstairs and into the spare room to watch them from the window as they made their way down the street. Within a minute or so, they had moved beyond her line of sight, and she slowly turned from the window, her gaze falling on the recovery charm hanging from the bedpost. Its fragrance no longer filled the room, and she removed it, noting with a smile that the room was tidy and Ethan had made the bed.

Her smile faded. She had lied to him. The gun was hidden in a box underneath her bed, but she hadn't wanted him to have it, was worried it would only encourage more violence. But it hadn't made a difference in the end. Mike had seen to that. She closed the bedroom door and made her way slowly downstairs.

She placed the recovery charm on the coffee table absently as she sat down. She wasn't sure what to make of Mike. Ethan's friend and partner, someone whom he trusted implicitly.

When she had taken his hand, she had been shaken by a wave of coldness, of negative energy. She had quickly withdrawn from him, trying to hide her unease and surprise. Perhaps it had been because he too was wary of her, not sure if he could trust her, and she had simply been picking up on his feelings. She had tried to read him as they talked, but she found it difficult; his aura was blurred and unclear, and she had the impression he was hiding from her, which was ridiculous; what reason did he have to hide?

She chewed her lip thoughtfully. Mike was clearly wary about trusting her, and she understood that. He was like Ethan in some ways, a product of his job: suspicious and unwilling to give his trust to anyone. Maybe she just needed to give him the benefit of the doubt. He'd come down here, hadn't he? Agreed to look into anything suspicious in the village?

Willow closed her eyes, trying to shut out the unsettling thoughts flying around her head. It might be hours before they got back, and she couldn't sit here fretting and second guessing what they might find. Needing to keep herself busy, she turned her attention to housework.

It was a small cottage and didn't take much cleaning, nor did she create much ironing. Nevertheless, it was a couple of hours later, just as she was coming downstairs after putting away the freshly ironed clothes, that a muffled thumping noise made her jump. Her eyes automatically swung to the wall separating her cottage from Alison's. The walls were thick enough to ensure little sound passed between the two houses, but that noise had been loud and definitely from next door. She held her breath, listening for any further sounds, but all was quiet, and after a while Willow decided it couldn't have been anything serious.

Going through to the kitchen to make herself a well-earned mug of coffee, she was filling the kettle with water from the kitchen tap when movement at the bottom of the garden caught her eye through the window. Her heart missed a beat when she saw someone running up the garden path but breathed a sigh of relief when she saw it was Alison. That relief turned to fear when her next-door neighbor hammered on the door as if the hounds of hell were after her.

"Willow! Willow, help me!" Her cries were slightly muted through the door, but there was no mistaking the panic in her voice.

Willow hurriedly unlocked the door and opened it, catching Alison as she almost fell through.

"What is it? What's wrong?" Her heart was thumping painfully in her chest, her breathing uneven as Alison's expression sent a lance of fear shooting through her. Was it something to do with Carter?

"It's Gary. He's fallen down the stairs," Alison managed, tears streaming down her face as she clutched at Willow. "I think…I think he might dead. Oh, please come and help me."

For a split second, Willow simply stared at her friend in horror, but then blinked and nodded, running down the path after Alison, back up the next-door garden and into the house. She paused in the doorway to take a calming breath. Her heart was beating so fast she thought she might faint, and that wouldn't be of any help to Alison.

She resisted her friend's clutching fingers as they pulled at her jumper, urging her toward the stairs between the kitchen and the living room. After a moment, she straightened her shoulders and allowed Alison to pull her through the kitchen, the layout a mirror image of her own house.

The sight of Gary's crumpled body, lying in a heap at the bottom of the stairs, brought her to a halt. Her stomach lurched and she closed her eyes, fighting to remain calm. After everything she had been through the last few days, and now this? She shook her head, trying to think straight, but it was difficult to think of anything over the sound of her friend's panicked wailing.

She turned to Alison, gripped her shoulders, and gave her a shake. "Stop it! I can't do this on my own. I need you to be calm for me. For Gary."

Alison's tear-filled eyes were wide and frightened, but as Willow continued to glare at her she grew quieter and nodded.

"Okay." Willow turned back to Gary and, after a brief hesitation, knelt by his side. There was no blood, no obvious signs of injury, and as she looked at him thought she saw his chest rise ever so slightly. Relief washed over her, and she leaned closer to press her fingers to his wrist, closing her eyes to better concentrate. His pulse beat strongly beneath her fingers, and he gave a slight groan at her touch.

"He's alive. Oh, thank God for that." She tipped her head back to the ceiling, blowing out a long breath.

Beside her, Alison threw herself on the floor next to her husband, and Willow put out a protective arm, pulling her back from Gary. "Wait, be careful. We need to check he hasn't broken anything."

Chapter Twelve

"Could she have brought you to a more remote place?" Mike shoved his hands in his pockets and hunched his shoulders as he scowled across at the snow-covered hills stretching up to meet the pale blue sky. It was still thawing, and the snow was turning to slush in places.

Ethan continued striding along the path toward the village center. "It's where she lives."

Mike wasn't impressed. "So come on, what happened?"

Ethan shook his head. "I don't know. It was all good; I thought I'd got Carter's trust…" He paused and then shook his head again. "No, I had got his trust, I know that. And then…boom, out of nowhere."

He looked at Mike, keeping pace with him as they strode along. "I was so close. I was almost there, ready to bring him in. I just don't get it."

"You didn't get a sense there was an insider in the Force?"

"Not a clue." He frowned uncertainly. "Maybe I was wrong. Maybe I didn't have Carter's trust after all. I mean, if I had, surely he would have told me about an insider."

"Well, you were right about one thing," Mike said. "You must have been getting too close for comfort, and the insider gave Carter the heads up."

He nodded but didn't say anything, and they continued in silence for a few minutes until once again Mike broke into his troubled thoughts. "So, what's the plan here?"

Ethan looked up, surprised to find they were nearing the village green. He drew to a halt and gathered his thoughts. "Okay, you see what you can find out from the shop, see if anyone has seen or heard anything about strangers in the village."

"Apart from the two of us, you mean?" Mike grinned, and Ethan responded with a reluctant smile. "So, what are you going to be doing?"

Ethan looked across at The Half Moon. "I'm going to have a few words with the landlord over there."

Mike raised an eyebrow. "You said that as if you meant it. Anything I should know about? Need any help?"

"No."

****

Warmth rushed to meet Ethan as he walked in through the storm porch and pushed open the door to the Lounge room. Last night it had been crammed, but this morning it couldn't have been more different, with only two customers nursing their drinks on the table in front of them. A fire crackled and snapped at the far end of the L shaped room, and in stark contrast to the loud festivities of last night the Half Moon now appeared to be a sanctuary of cozy warmth and calm. Dark wood furniture with ruby red velour seats and a faded maroon carpet gave the room a slightly dated but nevertheless comfortable ambience.

He nodded to the two customers sitting by the fire and walked across to the bar. Sam appeared from the back room, his face lighting up in recognition as he saw Ethan. "Now then," he said, cheerfully. "Come for a hair of the dog, is it?"

As friendly as you like, thought Ethan. Sam's duplicity jarred his tightly held temper. "No. I wouldn't mind a quick chat, though."

"Oh, aye?"

"First things first." He pulled out a piece of paper from his pocket. "Do me a favor? Will you write down The Half Moon's address for me?"

"Ah, I'll be hoping you're giving me a good review on my website, then?" Sam dutifully wrote down the address before handing the paper back to Ethan, who carefully folded it and put it back in his pocket.

"Thanks. Appreciate it."

"You wanted a word about something?"

"I'd like to talk Christmas cards."

Sam's usually ruddy face drained of color, leaving two bright spots high on his cheekbones, and he cast a quick glance toward the couple by the fire. "How about we talk through the back there?" He gestured through the door leading to the pub's living quarters.

"I'm easy. Wherever you like." Ethan smiled grimly; Sam's obvious fear gave him a sense of satisfaction.

"Aye, aye, let's go through the back there."

Sam lifted the bar hatch to allow him through and then ushered him into the kitchen, moving from one foot to the other distractedly as Ethan calmly pulled out a chair and sat at the table.

Sam continued to pace nervously. "Can I get you a drink?"

"I'm not thirsty." Ethan gestured to the chair opposite. "Why don't you take a seat?"

Sam did as he was told, sitting forward with his forearms on the table, clasping and unclasping his hands and refusing to meet his gaze. Ethan wasn't inclined to break the silence and simply looked at Sam with interest. The color had returned to his face, and beads of sweat shone on his upper lip. His breathing was unsteady, and he was going to make his hands sore if he continued to wring them as he was doing. It was Sam who eventually broke the silence.

He didn't glance up, didn't meet Ethan's gaze. "So, what was it you wanted to talk about?"

"I want to know why you did it."

Sam risked a quick glance, flinched at what he saw in Ethan's face, and dropped his gaze once again. "Did what? I don't know what you're talking about."

Ethan leaned forward, resting his own forearms on the table. "Don't play games with me because I'm telling you now you'll regret it. Now, I have a sample of your handwriting right here in my pocket. And Willow has kept every single one of those cards you wrote, along with the envelopes, which will contain your DNA. So, I'll ask you again. Why did you do it?"

Sam's face once again paled as he finally looked up and met Ethan's gaze.

****

Ethan left the pub ten minutes later, confident Willow wasn't going to have any further problems with Sam. He saw Mike leaning against the shop wall and walked over to him.

"Everything all right?" Mike was clearly curious.

"All sorted," said Ethan with a grim smile. "What about you? Any luck?"

He gave a disparaging snort. “Asked around in the shop, along all these houses around the green. No one has seen a thing. As expected.”

Ethan ignored him. He wasn’t overly surprised, but unlike Mike he didn’t think that necessarily meant there hadn’t been anyone hanging around. He turned slowly in a circle, looking for anything that tugged at his consciousness, pulled at his instinct. He pointed down the road leading out of the village, the road that was now open.

“Let’s have a little wander down there.”

Mike opened his mouth as if to protest but in the end simply shrugged and once more fell into step beside his partner. They had not gone far before the row of houses ended, but Ethan kept on, curious about the low stone building a little farther down the road. As they neared the building, he saw it was derelict, with holes in the gray slate roof. It had obviously been used for storage at one point but had clearly not been used for many years. He slowly walked around to the side of the building, the side facing away from the village. Mike followed him curiously.

“What is it you’re looking for?”

Ethan pointed to the tire tracks in the snow. “A vehicle has been parked up here.”

“So?”

“So, who would be parking here? There are no houses this far down the road, and no one from the village would have reason to park here.”

“How do you know that?” Mike reasoned. “There might be good reason for someone to park down here. Taking their dog for a walk, leaving their car here while they went to the pub last night…anything.”

Ethan shook his head. "No. Someone parked here, deliberately out of sight, and then walked into the village, to the Half Moon."

Mike pulled off his hat and dragged a hand through his hair, breathing out a long breath. "Ethan, you're reaching, and you know it."

"You're saying Willow is lying, and she's somehow part of this thing?"

"I'm saying you need to consider it," snapped Mike. "Any other case and we wouldn't be having this conversation, and you know it. You've got yourself too close to this, and you're refusing to consider a key line of enquiry."

Fighting the urge to punch his partner in the face, Ethan turned and strode down the road, taking long, deep breaths in an effort to control his temper. The snow was piled high along either side of the road where Jonathan's snowplow had cleared a narrow path; it was barely wide enough for a car to get through. He stood, hands on hips, staring down at the snow covering his boots, and focusing on his breathing, but it was a good few minutes before he felt in control enough to walk back to Mike.

"Okay." He paused and took another breath. "So, give me your theory."

"You going to listen?"

"Yeah, I'm going to listen."

Mike gave him a searching look as if to make sure and then nodded. "Okay. So, Carter learns you're an undercover cop, arranges to have you killed. Only trouble is, he knows you, knows it won't be easy. So, he arranges for two of his goons to do the job, but needs a backup, a contingency plan in case things get tricky, which is likely. He posts a couple of people at different exits, just in case."

"Now who's reaching?"

"I've done a bit of digging, Ethan. Your girl went to university in York, was there the same time as Carter. Maybe not so much of a reach after all."

Mike held up his hand as Ethan opened his mouth to respond. "So, she brings you back here. She was a back-up, that's all, a runner, not really into doing the dirty work, so she just needs to keep you here until Carter can finish the job."

Anger and irritation burned the back of Ethan's throat. Mike's explanation was plausible, but he didn't believe it. Willow wasn't any part of this.

"So why isn't he here then? Why hasn't he come to finish the job?"

Mike shrugged. "There's no rush. Willow's doing a fine job of keeping you here. Suggests a few near misses with someone hanging around, knows you feel responsible for her safety, knows you won't leave while there's a chance she's in danger, so she creates that danger. Meanwhile, Carter might have her try and find out who you've told what, what intel you've passed on that he needs to know about."

"I'm not buying it."

They were almost back at the cottage, and Ethan quickened his step, not caring to listen to any more of Mike's theories. Pushing open the gate, he walked down the path and knocked on the door.

When there was no reply, he knocked again, turning to flash his partner a worried glance as Mike sauntered down the path.

"Willow? Willow, it's me. Open the door." He banged on the front door with the palm of his hand, listening for any sign of movement from within. Stepping across to the window, he leaned close, cupping his hands to combat the reflection of pale clouds in the glass. The living room was empty, and he blew out a quick breath, his heart rate quickening in sudden fear. He had told her not to leave, not to open the door to anyone. Where was she?

Pushing past Mike, he ran back down the path and along the pavement to the end of the terrace and down along to the back. Reaching the gate to Willow's back garden, he glanced up the path. The kitchen door was open. His heart missed a beat, and his knees sagged, causing him to stumble slightly as he glanced at Mike.

Mike reached for his firearm, nodding for Ethan to go ahead. He hurried down the path and entered the kitchen, his glance taking in Willow's boots by the door as always. They made their way quickly and efficiently through the house, Ethan's heart pounding harder in his chest with every room they found empty. She wasn't there.

****

Gary lay on the sofa with no injuries other than a sore head, a twisted ankle, and a few bruises, the biggest of which was to his ego. He was acutely embarrassed that Alison had enlisted Willow's help and although grateful clearly wished her to leave so he could nurse his wounded pride in private. With assurances that Laura was on her way to ensure there were no more serious injuries, Willow took her leave and quietly closed the back door.

It was only then she realized she still wore her fluffy slippers, much the worse for wear now, not having fared well with the run through the snowy garden. Retracing her steps back to her own cottage in a more composed manner, she trudged up the path and into the kitchen. She kicked off the ruined slippers and pushed the door closed behind her, leaning back against it wearily and closing her eyes.

"Where the hell were you?"

Her eyes flew open, and she pressed her back against the door as Ethan strode in from the living room. He grasped her shoulders, his fingers digging in painfully. "I told you to stay here. To keep the doors locked. Where were you?"

"You're hurting me."

He radiated anger and fear, and she tried to ease herself from his grip. For a moment she thought he hadn't heard, but then he released her so abruptly her knees threatened to buckle.

"Ethan." Mike appeared behind him to put a hand on his partner's shoulder. Ethan's intense gaze didn't waver from Willow, and she was held captive by the intensity of his dark scrutiny. Without a word he spun away from her into the living room.

"Are you all right?" Mike's voice was calm and quiet, his eyes cold. When she nodded, he continued. "You'll have to excuse my partner. He's a little upset. More than I've ever seen him, to be honest. Which is interesting." He stared at her in silence before gesturing to the table. "Why don't we have a little chat?"

She tried to block the cold negativity emanating from him, cold negativity, and something else she didn't want to identify. He didn't move until she inched her way to the table and sat down. Only then did he take the seat opposite.

"Where were you?"

"I was only next door," she whispered, swallowing painfully against a suddenly dry throat.

He looked at her, his head on one side. "And why did you decide to go next door? Why did you leave the house when Ethan had expressly asked you not to? Why leave the back door open, not take any coat or boots? Why did you generally leave the house in such a way as to suggest you might have been, oh I don't know, taken against your will? Why did you do that?"

She stared at him in dawning realization. She saw it was exactly how it must have appeared to them when they returned home. She had been in such a hurry to help Alison that she hadn't thought of anything other than to get to Gary as quickly as possible.

"I'm so sorry. I didn't think." She forgot her unease, and leaned forward, thinking only of what Ethan must have felt when he found her missing. "Alison came to the back door in such a state. Gary had fallen down the stairs and was unconscious. She thought he was dead and…and I just rushed across to try and help. I didn't think."

She looked up to see Ethan standing in the doorway. "I'm so sorry. I know what you said but…but she thought he was dead. I had to help her."

He closed his eyes and dropped his head forward with a soft laugh. "Of course, you did." He looked back up at her, his expression unreadable. "Because that's what you do."

She pushed herself from the table and walked across to him, lifting a tentative hand to his chest. "I'm sorry."

When he didn't move, she stepped into him and wrapped her arms around his waist, her head on his chest. She felt him shaking. After a moment he put his arms around her, and she breathed a sigh of relief.

"So, tell me. I'm assuming Gary wasn't dead?"

She laughed against his chest. "No. He'd knocked himself out, but we managed to get him onto the sofa, and he doesn't appear to have any major injuries. Alison called Laura; she's on her way to make sure."

"How very convenient."

Willow stiffened at the tone of Mike's voice and took a step to move from Ethan's embrace, but his arms tightened around her.

"Give it a rest, Mike."

"What? You believe that crap?"

Ethan dropped his arms and leaned back to search Willow's face, running a finger along her jawline before turning to Mike. "Yes, I do. If you don't, you're more than welcome to call in on them next door to check."

With that, he caught hold of Willow's hand and pulled her through into the living room.

Chapter Thirteen

"I…he what?" Willow stared at him in disbelief.

"I went to see him. He admitted it."

"No…no you're wrong, Sam wouldn't do that." She blinked away the wave of dizziness enveloping her. After everything that had happened, this was just too much. Her vision blurred as tears filled her eyes, and she swallowed hard. "He didn't…"

Ethan reached out to gently brush the tears from her cheeks. "That's the second time I've made you cry. I'm sorry."

She dashed away her tears with the palm of her hand. "I can't believe it."

He gave a lopsided smile. "He was mortified, if it helps. Said it was a moment of madness. He still… cares about you. Finding out I was staying here brought out the green-eyed monster, it seems."

"But it doesn't make any sense." She was unable to process Ethan's words. "If he cares about me, why would he do something so horrible?

"And was it Sam who followed us? Was he the one in the hoodie?"

She found that even harder to believe. The black energy emanating from that man had been something else; whatever Sam had done she had never sensed anything so negative from him.

Ethan frowned. "He denied it but—"

"Yes, it was." Mike broke into their conversation, irritation sharpening his voice as he leaned against the kitchen door frame. "There is no other explanation. There has been no stranger stalking through the village. It was either your bloody ex or…"

Willow flinched. He had not said a word up to now, simply watched her with an expression that told her he clearly didn't believe her. Well, that was nothing new. Mike didn't believe anything she said or did. Why was that, she wondered? What had she done to earn such distrust?

"It was either my ex…or I was making it up." She lifted her chin in defiance. "That's what you were going to say, wasn't it?"

The corner of Mike's mouth lifted, and he raised an eyebrow. "You said it."

"Back off, Mike." Ethan's voice was cold, and it clearly riled his partner, because he threw them both a look of disgust and retreated into the kitchen.

Deliberately avoiding Ethan's glance, she picked at a loose thread on her skirt. "You can say I told you so."

He frowned. "Why would I do that?"

"Because it's true." Her chin trembled slightly. "From the first moment I met you, you've said I'm too trusting. I guess you're right. I am."

"You are the most trusting person I've ever met. But here, in this village? Who's to say that's a bad thing?" He ducked his head to look at her. "You're also warm, and open, and honest. And if you were any different, I might not be alive today." He gave a crooked smile. "I don't have any right to say I told you so."

Willow looked up at him, feeling her stomach quiver as he returned her stare. She wanted him so much, needed him even. She was about to reach across to touch his arm when he pulled away as if reading her thoughts, and she sensed his withdrawal from her.

They'd found nothing in the village, no one who had seen or heard anything unusual, no mystery stranger. No reason for Ethan to stay.

"You're leaving." She tried a smile, not sure if it worked or not. "No reason to stay here and protect me now you've solved the mystery."

Ethan hesitated, but then nodded. "Maybe."

"Look, sorry to interrupt." Mike was back in the doorway, clearly not sorry in the least. "We're wasting time. We need to talk about how we're going to play this when we get back."

Willow immediately got to her feet. "Then I'll leave you both to it."

She paused in front of Mike, waiting for him to step aside and allow her through. After a moment, he leaned to one side, barely leaving her room to brush past him in the doorway. She closed her eyes as a blast of negative energy shivered down her spine. It was with some relief that she closed the door on the both of them.

How could she have been so wrong about Sam? She would have staked her life on him having nothing to do with those hateful cards. They were friends…well, she had thought they were friends.

Willow gripped the back of one of her kitchen chairs, chewing her lip. She and Sam had been out a few times, but it hadn't lasted for more than a few months before she had ended it. That had been well over three years ago, and although things had been awkward for a little while they had eventually settled into an easy friendship. She swallowed an uncomfortable feeling in the back of her throat; Sam clearly wasn't who she thought he was. Ethan had seen through him straight away, why hadn't she?

Moving to the cupboards, she pulled open first one door, then another, not sure what she was looking for but unable to keep still. Turning away, her gaze fell on her boots standing by the door, and she was suddenly overwhelmed by the need for fresh air and wide-open spaces.

Without pausing to think any further, she pulled on her boots, coat, and hat, and let herself out of the back door, closing it behind her and making her way out onto the road. She turned left, away from the village, taking the same route she had with Ethan that first morning. But instead of walking through to the end of the village, she turned off onto the public footpath up to the field where families usually went sledging.

Standing by the gate, her gaze lifted to the copse of trees at the top of the steep, sloping field. To her relief, it was deserted; no one was out sledging. The trees were bare except for the rookery nests dotted among the skeletal branches, as if the trees were carefully holding the precious nests and keeping them safe; the rooks themselves wheeled and dived through the sky. Willow envied them their freedom. It was cold and bright, and she breathed in deeply, trying to calm her thoughts, but they continued to whirl around her head, mirroring the flight of the birds up above. Ethan, Mike, Gary, Ethan, Sam, Carter, Ethan…

Despite the chill winter air, she felt as if she was burning up inside, confused and uncertain, unable to believe the speed with which her life had suddenly turned upside down. With an inarticulate cry of frustration, she started to run up the hill, pushing on through the snow as if she could escape her thoughts. As she got farther up the field, the incline and the snow impeded her progress, and she struggled to maintain her headlong flight, catching her foot in a drift and pitching forward.

For a few long moments, she simply lay there unmoving, welcoming the cold snow beneath her burning face, closing her eyes and wondering if she could just fall asleep and wake up to find this had all been a dream. The next moment, someone grabbed the back of her coat and hauled her upright. Gasping in surprise, she spun around.

"Mike!"

His only response was to grab her arm, his grip painful even through the thickness of her coat. She tried to pull free, but his fingers tightened. His gaze was icy, without a hint of expression, and once again Willow sensed the negative energy pulsing from him.

He leaned closer, and his mouth curved into a grin. "You are playing a blinder, missy. I couldn't plan this any better if I tried."

"What do you mean?" She struggled against his grip but was unable to free herself. His gaze lifted from hers to glance over her shoulder for a split second before returning to her when she spoke again. "Let me go."

"And just where were you running to?" he demanded, roughly, pulling her closer. "Carter's gang? Is that who you were running to? Going to get a message to him?"

Willow stopped struggling, her mouth open in horror. "What are you talking about?"

"Your innocent act won't wash with me. You haven't got me wrapped around your little finger like my partner here."

Ethan appeared from behind her, his eyes narrowed on them both, breathing hard from exertion and wincing with pain. "Willow—"

"Where is it?" Mike interrupted, leaning forward until his face was just inches from hers. "Where's your phone? You going to give them an update?"

"You're being ridiculous," she spat as he searched her pockets with his other hand. When he withdrew a phone triumphantly from her pocket, she made a grab for it but cried out in pain when he tightened his grip on her arm.

"Stop!" Ethan stepped forward immediately, his hand on Mike's arm. "Let her go."

"She's lying." Mike didn't take his eyes from her. He held out the phone to Ethan. "Why don't you take a look? See who she's been making calls to?"

"I haven't! I just needed some air. That's all, I swear. This is crazy."

"Let her go. Now."

There was a steely edge to Ethan's voice, and after a moment Mike pushed her away from him in disgust. He turned to thrust his face into his partner's. "For fuck's sake, Ethan. Get a grip. You're thinking with your dick. She's playing you for a fool."

He spun away and strode back down the hill. Ethan watched him go, his expression thoughtful, before turning back to Willow, frowning when he saw her massaging her arm.

Gaze wary, he kept his distance. "You okay? Did he hurt you?"

“I’m okay.” She managed a smile. What was happening? Everything was changing, and she didn’t like the uncertainty in Ethan’s eyes. “Please tell me you don’t believe him. I just needed to get outside; after everything that’s happened, I just needed some air.”

After a moment, he nodded, the tension visibly leaving his shoulders. “Come on. Let’s get back.”

“Ethan. I don’t trust him. Something’s not right.”

His expression immediately darkened, and he muttered an explicit curse under his breath “What is it with you two? He doesn’t trust you; you don’t trust him. Well, I trust you both. You’d better get used to it.”

He was about to turn away when Willow caught his arm. She had to get through to him. “I mean it, Ethan. You can’t trust him.”

He stared at her, his eyes hard, and then moved closer. “I’ve known him for five years. I’ve known you for less than a week. Don’t make me choose.”

His words cast a chill of fear through her, and her breath stilled in her throat as he walked away, his movements stiff and angry. Whereas ten minutes earlier she had felt as if she was burning up, now cold seeped through her, spreading from within. She swallowed against the lump in her throat, hunching her shoulders against the chill before slowly walking back down the hill and toward home.

****

Ethan watched Mike walk away from him, aware of the anger his partner was trying hard to control. He had always had a quick temper, but it was rarely directed at him. He blew out a long breath, unable to understand why Mike had taken against Willow so badly; it made him uneasy.

Willow.

He closed his eyes. He'd been hard on her but was frustrated by the pair of them and didn't like playing piggy in the middle. Looking up, he saw her coming through the gate in the field, surprise flickering across her face when she saw him waiting for her. The surprise turned to wariness, and his heart sank; he didn't blame her. She'd had to put up with a lot in the last few days.

He held out his hand as she drew near, but she ignored it.

"I'm sorry. I shouldn't have lost my temper." He gave a half-smile and held up the phone he'd taken from Mike. "Here."

She took the phone from him. "Have you checked it? Seen if I've made any suspicious calls or texts?"

He frowned in surprise. Did she really think he would? "Of course not."

She stared at the phone and then looked up with an odd expression. She held it out toward him. "This isn't my phone. I've never seen it before."

He hesitated before taking the phone from her and pressing the home key. The keypad flashed into view, requiring a passcode. "Mike took this from your pocket."

"It's not mine," she repeated quietly. "He obviously put it there."

Ethan closed his eyes. Was it possible Mike had put it there deliberately, or had he simply dropped his phone when they were tussling in the snow? What the hell was going on? Nothing made any sense anymore.

He opened his eyes and saw Willow looking at him uncertainly, saw her drop her gaze again. "Where is Mike anyway?"

He held out his hand once more. “He’s gone to speak to the Chief, see if we can bring in Carter. We agreed I’ll stay here just to be sure.”

“To make sure I’m not going to warn Carter?”

“That’s his reason. It’s not mine.” He held her gaze, read the doubt in her eyes, but her trusting nature meant she took his hand anyway. They turned and walked back toward the village; she trusted him implicitly. That thought stilled the breath in his throat, and he drew to a halt, suddenly uneasy with the path his thoughts were taking.

She looked up at him in surprise. “What is it?”

“You’re too trusting. I’ve said it so often, and yet from the first moment, you didn’t trust Mike.” He searched her face. “Why?”

Willow shook her head unhappily and tried unsuccessfully to pull her hand from his. “Please. I don’t want to argue anymore.”

“I’m not arguing,” he said, softly. “I’m being serious. You trust everyone. What is it about Mike? I saw it in your face the moment you shook his hand. What was it?”

He caught her other hand and turned her to face him; her hands felt small and cold in his, despite her gloves. She stood before him, unmoving in the snow, her head bowed. He gave her time until eventually she took a deep breath as if coming to a decision. She looked up at him, her eyes clear.

“Coldness. Negativity. Something…” She frowned as if unable to put it into words. “I don’t know how to explain it but later it was as if he was hiding from me…mentally, not physically.”

“Hiding what?”

Willow shrugged. “I don’t know. He doesn’t trust me, hasn’t done even before he met me, when you first told him how you’d escaped that night. Maybe I was just picking up on his distrust…”

“Maybe.” He felt her hands shivering in his. “Come on, you’re freezing. Let’s go home.”

When they arrived back at Willow’s cottage, Mike’s truck was gone, leaving nothing but a pair of tire tracks in the snow on the road. Ethan stared at them with a sense of unease. Something was pulling at his consciousness, but it danced just beyond his reach. He stifled a sigh; he agreed with Willow’s view that Mike had made up his mind before he came. The problem was, what to do about it? She had already become far too involved in this case, and he didn’t want her getting dragged in any deeper.

Chapter Fourteen

Ethan awoke the next morning feeling far from refreshed; he'd slept fitfully, tossing and turning as he tried to decide the best way of handling things. He trusted Mike but wasn't sure he trusted him not to overplay his prejudice against Willow when he put his case to the Chief, particularly after that stunt with the phone.

At the same time, he couldn't ignore the potential threat of the hooded stranger; despite Mike's assertions, he still wasn't convinced it was Sam. He was torn, and his fear for Willow was tying him in knots. Either way, he couldn't win.

Willow was equally quiet and thoughtful as they ate their breakfast in silence until, unable to stand it any longer, he pushed his chair away from the table. She looked up in surprise. "Come on, let's get out of here."

Ten minutes later, they were striding down the path toward the village center, their breath swirling in front of them in the chill morning air.

"You said something about this being part of the Yorkshire Wolds Way?" He stared straight ahead, making an effort to break the silence still hanging between them.

From the corner of his eye, he saw the oversized fluffy ball on her hat bobbing as she nodded. It brought a smile to his lips and lightened his mood, and he breathed in the sharp, cold air, feeling it fill his lungs.

"Yes, it brings in a fair amount of trade through the summer months, which really helps…" She took a deep breath and carried on. "Sam…and Jane in the village shop. The walk just touches the far end of the village, we can pick it up just before the track to Jonathan's farm. I'm not sure how far we'll be able to go today, though. It depends how much the snow has melted."

"Well, we can give it a go."

She slowed a little as they neared the tiny village green, the large Christmas tree standing tall and proud, and he saw her cast a wary glance to the left where The Half Moon stood.

Ethan pulled her closer to him as they continued to walk toward the green. "Don't think about it," he said, squeezing her fingers through her gloves. He stopped across from the green and stood looking at the Christmas tree. It was just past ten in the morning, and the sun was having difficulty breaking through the heavily overcast sky. The slight breeze brought with it wisps of snow, whirling around them.

The Half Moon and the village shop looked warm and inviting with their Christmas lights twinkling in the windows. Colored lights hung in the windows of the little row of terraced houses facing the green, adding to the picture-perfect scene.

"Brigadoon," he murmured with a smile as he looked down at Willow. "This place really does look too good to be true."

"It is too good to be true, isn't it?" The uncharacteristic bitterness in her voice shocked him.

"Hey." He frowned, and caught her chin with his finger, lifting her gaze to his. "This is still your home, nothing has changed; it's still the place you love." He shook his head, trying to find the right words. "People do stupid things sometimes. Sam did a stupid thing, but he won't do anything like that again. Don't let it spoil this place for you."

She nodded unhappily, clearly unconvinced, but allowed Ethan to take her hand and pull her away from the green.

"Come on, show me where this walk is."

Half an hour later, she paused to catch her breath, having made it up the snow-covered path to where it met the woods halfway up the valley side. The snow was far lighter here under the shelter of the trees, and she drew in a long, deep breath.

"That was some climb." Ethan bent over, his hands on his knees as he too caught his breath. As he straightened, he winced and held a hand to his side. "I'm out of shape. That should have been a walk in the park."

She raised her eyebrows. "A walk in the park? Hardly. The snow made it pretty tough going, but even in the summer not many people would call that a walk in the park."

He grinned. "You're probably right." He looked around him, his eyes following the path as it zig-zagged and snaked its way through the woods, continuing its upward journey to the top of the valley.

The path had a much lighter covering of snow, but the steady incline made it no less challenging, and halfway up to the top, Ethan paused by one of the rough, wooden benches and brushed the snow from the seat. They sat in companionable silence for a few minutes, listening to the calming sounds of animals rustling through the undergrowth, birds chattering in the trees far above them, and of the snow shifting and falling from the skeletal branches as it melted.

"Oh, I do love it here." She closed her eyes and smiled. "Whenever I come up here, I try and come at a time when I don't think anyone else will be around, which is difficult in the summer. But when I do, it feels like time stops. I can come here and just…be."

Her eyes snapped open, and she looked at Ethan fiercely as if daring him to mock her, but he didn't, he simply nodded, a small smile lifting the corner of his mouth.

"I can see it," he said softly. He reached across to brush a wayward strand of hair that had escaped from her woolen hat. "You belong here."

He saw it. Saw how she was completely at home, that she did indeed belong here. And there was something magical about this place. Even he was able to sense the energy, feel its invigorating power. He was calmer now; the walk, or this place, had cleared his head, and he had made his decision; he would go back to York today and speak to the Chief and Mike. In the cold light of day, he considered the risk to Willow was minimal. Carter was the risk, and if they brought him in swiftly, she was safe.

It felt good to have made the decision, and yet the thought of never coming here again, never sitting by Willow's side, filled him with a deep sadness. He shook his head as if to dispel the thought, surprised by his visceral reaction to this place. Just a short time left. He glanced at her with an ache in his throat; she was lost in her own thoughts.

"Have you always lived here?"

His voice made her jump, and she blinked. "Um, sort of. I grew up in a village a few miles away, so I've always lived around here. I went to the University of York to do my teacher training but always wanted to come back, and I was lucky enough to get a teaching job here in the village."

"What about your parents?"

She gave a soft laugh. "As soon as I was settled with a job and a house, my parents sold up, bought a camper van, and have been traveling the world ever since." She laughed harder as he raised his eyebrows in surprise. "They're having the time of their life. It was always their dream; they were just waiting for Patrick and me to be in a position where we weren't dependent on them. I think it's fantastic."

"Ah yes, Patrick, your brother." Ethan tugged the collar of his Parker. "Whom I have to thank for lending me his coat."

She nodded. "Yes, he's in New Zealand. Went out in his gap year and stayed there. He runs a successful scuba diving business, mainly for tourists. He's fairly settled there."

His gaze was gentle but curious. "You're a homebody in a family of adventurers."

"I never really thought of it like that," said Willow with a surprised smile. "But yes, I suppose I am."

"Do you miss them?" He asked. "Your family?"

"Sometimes." She thought about it, her head on one side. "A little. I Skype with them a lot, and they're all having such an amazing time, but I don't envy them. I love what I do and where I live. I love my life here. I've been out to see Patrick a couple of times, and it's been great to see him, but I'm so glad to come back home. And they all come back home here at least once a year, so we're still pretty close. You know, I have a few friends whose family live just a few miles from them, and they don't see or speak to them as much as I do to mine."

She pulled a face. "It sounds as if I'm trying to justify it to you, but I'm not. I feel really close to my family."

When Ethan simply nodded, she gently elbowed him. "So, what about you? Your family?"

He shrugged. "Well, I guess you can tell I'm a Southerner by my accent." He gave her a sideways glance with a smile. "I grew up in Cirencester with my parents and brother, Jake. Mum is a nurse, Dad is in the police, and Jake is a GP. No adventurers in the family, I'm afraid."

"But you all help people," she said softly. "Do you see them often?"

"I go back once or twice a year; usually for birthdays, things like that. I'm usually working Christmas, but I tend to go back in between Christmas and New Year." He glanced at her with a wink. "And, like the good son I am, I ring my mother every couple of weeks or so."

She must worry about you. She didn't say it, but he heard it as clear as day when she looked at him. But then she smiled. "I'm very glad to hear it."

"Well," he said after a moment, pushing himself reluctantly from the bench, he turned to hold out a hand. "I guess we'd better be getting back."

As they reached the village green once more, Ethan's gaze was drawn down the road leading out of the village, his eyes seeking and settling on the old derelict stone building that he and Mike had walked to yesterday. He frowned, chewing his lip thoughtfully. There was still something niggling at the back of his mind, something that refused to go away but equally refused to fully reveal itself.

"What is it?" Willow was looking at him curiously.

He hesitated before deciding to listen to the voice in his head, the voice that told him there was something he was missing. "Let's just walk up here a bit."

Once again, he walked around to the side of the building facing away from the village. The chill air and lack of traffic meant the snow hadn't melted, and the tire tracks were still visible, evidencing that a vehicle had been parked there. She looked at him expectantly, and he pointed to the tracks.

"Do people regularly park here? Maybe to walk the dog? Something like that?"

Momentarily surprised, she looked at the space beside the old building, looked along the road, and then back toward the village, wrinkling her nose. "I can't say I've ever really noticed cars parking here, although it's not to say they don't. But people generally park in The Half Moon—it's a large carpark for such a small village, and Sam doesn't mind people parking there. People tend to walk up toward Jonathan's farm, and up onto the Wolds Way, or back up the hill we were on yesterday where there is a bridle path, but not really down along this road, to be fair. It's not the best route for a walk here."

He nodded, and Willow looked down at the tire tracks again. “Are you thinking it might have been whoever was following us?”

He shook his head. “I don’t know. It could have been anyone.”

He caught her hand in his once more, forcing a smile and pulling her with him as he began walking back to the village. “The answer isn’t going to slap us in the face standing here though, is it?”

****

Willow stared through the window, listening to Ethan moving around in the spare room upstairs. She tried to ignore the ache in her throat, not quite able to believe she would never see him again. Straightening her shoulders when she heard him coming down the stairs, she turned to face him as he came into the room. He put down his duffel bag and stood just inside the doorway.

“Well, I guess this is it.”

Despite her best intentions, she was unable to speak and shrugged her shoulders, dropping her gaze to hide her tear-filled eyes.

“Willow.”

She shook her head but lifted her chin to meet his gaze. “Will I ever see you again?” Her voice trembled but didn’t break.

Ethan hesitated, a frown creasing his forehead. “I don’t think so,” he said eventually.

She couldn’t just let him walk away. “But why? You feel it too, I know you do.”

“Willow, you know why. I—”

She ran across the room and flung her arms around his shoulders, burying her face into his neck and sobbing against him as his arms immediately tightened around her.

"I don't want you to go," she whispered, lifting her head to trail soft kisses along his neck, his jaw, his cheek, and eventually his mouth.

He shook with the effort it took to remain unresponsive, but as her lips met his a wordless sound of need escaped his throat. He pulled her closer, his mouth desperately seeking hers as his hands moved to cup her face. His kisses were fierce and full of longing until eventually he pulled away from her, his eyes closed, shudders wracking his body as he fought for control.

"This isn't real," he whispered, resting his forehead against hers.

"This doesn't feel real to you?" Willow kissed him again, but he pulled away just enough to break the kiss.

"Don't…don't….Willow. I can't…"

I can't stay. I can't leave.

He opened his eyes, his fingertips tracing a trembling line along her cheekbone, and she saw his agony, heard it, felt it, and was rocked with an answering pain. It was tearing him apart.

She nodded, although it went against every fiber of her being, and reached up to cup his face, his features blurring as tears filled her eyes. She carefully kissed his cheek and then stepped back from him with a reasonable attempt at a smile.

"I'm sorry, that wasn't fair." She dropped her eyes to the floor. "I know you have to leave."

His gaze burned. "Will you be all right?"

She straightened her shoulders then lifted her chin. She took two more steps back from him, needing to physically put some distance between them to stop herself from once more throwing herself at him. “Of course, I will. This is me. In my little cottage. I’ll be fine.” She even managed a light laugh. “And you do know this isn’t really Brigadoon, don’t you? We don’t all disappear as soon as you walk out of the village. If you ever change your mind, we’ll all still be here. It’s not a now or never moment.”

Ethan dropped his head and gave a half laugh. “That’s good to know.” He looked back up at her, his gray eyes searching her face as if committing her features to memory. “I can’t ever thank you enough. You saved my life.”

She waved his words away with an airy hand. “Oh pfft. You’ve added a little excitement in my otherwise quiet and provincial life. Now go on, go. And be careful with my little car.”

“I will. And I’ll arrange for it to be returned to you as soon as I can. With the wing mirror fixed.” He bent to lift his bag, shrugging it over one shoulder. “I haven’t been able to get hold of Mike yet, but we’ll get this sorted. They’ll probably need a statement from you, but…someone will be in touch about that.”

“It won’t be you?”

He hesitated. “Look, if you ever need anything, if you need to, you can contact me through Mike. You have his number.”

She nodded wordlessly. Mike’s number; not his. She went to her carved wooden cabinet and picked up the car keys she had left there earlier, handing them to Ethan without quite meeting his eyes. He looked at the little hessian bag tied to the keyring alongside a small silver amulet and then back at her.

“A protection charm.” She walked through to the kitchen, pulled open the door, and stood back to let him pass. “Goodbye, Ethan.”

After a brief hesitation, he cupped her cheek with one hand and kissed her, a brief, fierce kiss, and then he was gone, striding down the path and letting himself out through the gate. As he reached for the garage door, Willow carefully closed the back door and sank into a chair at the kitchen table. He was gone.

Chapter Fifteen

Willow glanced at her watch. One o'clock; two hours since Ethan left.

Two hours in which she had torn through the cottage like a cyclone, stripping the bed in the spare room and shoving the bedding in the washing machine, trying to remove all traces of him. She'd gone through the house systematically tidying and cleaning, and now she turned down the music she had put on at an ear-splittingly loud level while she cleaned, desperate to not give herself any capacity for thinking about him and for once not caring if she disturbed Alison and Gary next door.

She looked at the folded piece of paper she had found on his pillow, with her name thankfully written in a black, spiky scrawl rather than the hateful neat capitals on the envelopes Sam had written. She hadn't read it, but now, with trembling fingers, she unfolded the paper and read the short note.

I don't know what I did to deserve you finding me that night, Willow, but it must have been something good. I don't believe in coincidences or fate, but something led you to me, and that something saved my life. You saved my life, probably in more ways than one. It would be so easy to stay, to give us a try, far easier than saying goodbye. But I have to. I don't belong in your world, and you certainly don't belong in mine. I've never known anyone so full of genuine goodness, and I would be so afraid of you losing yourself in my world. Don't ever change, Willow Daniels, my guardian angel. Ethan.

She closed her eyes and allowed the tears to fall, then brought the note to her lips, placing a kiss on his name. After carefully refolding the note and placing it in the bottom drawer of her cabinet, she walked through to the kitchen, pulling open first the fridge and then cupboard doors, mentally checking off ingredients. She needed to keep busy. Mince pies. They would sell well at the Christmas Fete tomorrow, lots of mince pies.

But she needed ingredients, and so she pulled on her boots, coat, and scarf and set off down to the village at a brisk pace. She slowed as she neared Gwen's house and after a moment's hesitation pushed open the gate and knocked on her door.

"Willow!" Gwen pulled open the door. "What a lovely surprise. Do you want to come in for tea?"

She immediately realized her mistake. A cup of tea with Gwen wasn't going to take her mind off Ethan, it would only remind her of him and of the night they had spent here during the storm.

"Oh, um, no, it's okay, Gwen," she stammered, bending down to fuss over Chappie. "I was just popping to the shops and wondered if you needed anything?"

Gwen bit her lip. "Well, actually, do you mind if I come with you? Only, I haven't been any farther than the garden since the storm. I've been so afraid I might slip and fall in the snow, but if I had someone to walk with, I think it would be all right?"

"That's fine. Shall we bring Chappie with us?"

Five minutes later she was once more walking down toward the village shop, only this time at a much more sedate pace and with Gwen hanging tightly onto her arm. Gradually, her friend relaxed as she realized the paths had been well cleared and gritted by someone from the village.

"Oh, it's really not as bad as I thought."

"No, it's fine now." Willow patted her arm. "I'm hoping we're not going to get any more snow, but the sky looks a bit grim, don't you think?"

"It does rather. Where's your young man today?" Gwen paused as Chappie stopped to explore some scent or other at the edge of the path.

Willow swallowed and kept her voice casual. "Oh, he's gone back home now the snow has cleared. He has to get back to work. And he's not my young man, you know. He's just a friend."

Gwen looked at her sharply. "Well, I don't believe that for a minute, my dear, but it's your business." Her voice softened as she continued to look at Willow. "Whatever is meant to be, will be. You know that as well as I do."

She gave a gentle tug on Chappie's lead, and he immediately returned to her side, allowing them to continue down the road. As they neared the village center, Willow's gaze was drawn to The Half Moon, and she stiffened on seeing Sam's familiar figure in the doorway. He raised a hand to wave at them, which she ignored but which Gwen returned. Clearly encouraged, he hurried across the snow-covered green toward them.

"Afternoon, Gwen, Willow." His voice was cheerful enough, but his gaze was wary. "Um, have you got a minute, Willow?" He reached out as if to touch her arm but in the end let it drop by his side.

"I'm afraid I haven't actually, Sam," she said coolly. "I'm in a bit of a hurry, if you don't mind."

Gwen looked surprised. "Oh, there's no hurry on my account. We're not in any rush, are we, Chappie?"

Willow remained silent, her lips clamped shut, eyes fixed firmly on the village Christmas tree just over Sam's shoulder. Her heart was thumping so hard in her chest she felt quite faint, and despite the chill air beads of sweat broke out on her upper lip.

"Please," Sam said quietly, this time he did reach out and touch her arm.

Gwen looked between the two of them, clearly sensing something wasn't quite right, but unsure what. "Well, I'll just pop into the shop; I'll be two minutes."

She walked quickly over the road, stopping briefly to tie Chappie's leash to the post outside before disappearing into the shop. As soon as she was out of sight, Willow snatched her arm from Sam's fingers.

"Get away from me." She started to walk away from him.

"Willow, please, just hear me out." He reached for her again but stepped back in surprise when she rounded on him angrily. He held up his hands, palms facing outward in a placating gesture. "Please. I just want to explain. To say I'm sorry. Just come into The Half Moon so we can talk."

His usually ruddy, cheerful face was pale, his expression taught and unhappy, and her anger dissipated. She folded her arms across her chest. "If you want to talk, we can talk here."

His shoulders sagged in relief, and he gave an eager smile. "Okay, okay that's fine." When Willow just stood there looking at him, he dropped his gaze, wringing his hands together, clearly uncertain how to begin. “I am so, so sorry.” He chanced a quick glance at her face, saw she remained unmoved, and looked down at the snow at his feet. “I don’t know what came over me. You know how much I care about you, Willow. I’d never hurt you. You must know that. “

He risked another glance, his face even paler if that was possible, and she caught a glimpse of tears in his eyes. She sensed his remorse was genuine, could feel the beginnings of sympathy welling inside her, and looked away, angry with herself, reluctant to forgive him so easily. Saying sorry didn’t make everything all right.

“How could you do something like that, Sam?” She surprised herself by asking the question foremost in her head. “If you care about me, why would you do something so horrible?”

“I don’t know,” he said, helplessly. He reached for her hands. “Please believe me. You can’t hate me more than I hate myself. I didn’t realize how much I still cared for you until I saw you with Ethan. I just…I don’t know…I just saw red. It’s no excuse, I know.”

“You frightened me,” she said quietly.

“I know. I know I did, and I’m so sorry,” he mumbled and then after a moment tried a wan smile. “If it makes you feel any better, Ethan scared the bejesus out of me yesterday morning. I reckon there’s not many as would dare to cross him. I thought he was going to kill me.”

Willow didn’t say anything, not trusting herself to think about Ethan let alone speak to Sam about him. “I wouldn’t have believed you capable of this. Sending cards, following me…”

He immediately shook his head. "Look, I told Ethan the same. I didn't follow you." He frowned, unable to meet her eyes. "I admit I sent the cards, but I didn't do no following."

She looked at him uncertainly. Was he telling the truth? Or was she simply being too trusting, as Ethan had always told her. Sam was still holding her hands, his expression shamefaced, and she suddenly felt sick. She'd had enough. Pulling her hands from his, she stepped away from him.

"I need to go."

"Will you forgive me?" He looked up at her hopefully, and Willow's stomach churned once more.

"I don't know, Sam. I just don't know."

She turned away and walked unsteadily to the shop.

****

Ethan shivered as he waited in the car. It was bitterly cold outside and not much warmer inside without the engine running. The garden center was busy, probably full of people buying last minute Christmas decorations, and he sighed, an uncomfortable knot of uneasiness lying heavy in the pit of his stomach. Mike wasn't answering his mobile, and Ethan was reluctant to go to the police station without first speaking to him, not when he still didn't know who the insider was. On his return to York yesterday, he had dropped Willow's car in for repair, retrieved his own car, personal laptop, and mobile phone from secure storage, and booked into a hotel. He had spent a long evening going through all the evidence he had collated and saved on his USB, periodically trying to contact Mike.

After a restless night, not knowing what else to do and getting to the point of desperation, he had telephoned the Detective Chief Inspector's office and managed to get him to agree to meet with him away from the station. The Chief hadn't been happy about the clandestine meeting but in the end had reluctantly agreed.

Ethan looked up as a silver BMW pulled into the garden center carpark, and as it drove past he recognized the DCI. Drawing in a sharp breath as he opened the car door, the chill air biting, Ethan approached his superior officer when he alighted from the car, wearing a stony-faced expression.

"DCI Harper, thank you for coming."

"This better be good, McCormick." Harper didn't look pleased. "I don't appreciate being summoned, and I don't appreciate all this cloak and dagger crap."

"I understand, sir." Ethan nodded. "But as I explained on the phone, I needed to speak to you away from the station."

The Chief's expression didn't change. "So, what's your plan? Cozy chat in the café there?"

"No, sir, it's too busy." He ignored his senior officer's sarcasm. "Probably best if we talk in the car?"

Ethan gestured to his car and for a moment thought Harper might refuse. However, after giving him a searching stare, he walked stiffly toward the car. Stifling a sigh, Ethan followed. Pulling the door closed behind him, he took a deep breath, trying to remember the speech he had been rehearsing, the one that didn't make him sound too paranoid.

"DS Stott told me you were MIA." The inspector surprised Ethan before he was able to gather his thoughts. "As welcome as it is to see you unharmed, I have to ask why you have seen fit to break cover and why you have not been reporting to DS Stott as per protocol."

"I…I…has Mike, um DS Stott, not spoken to you yet?" Ethan was thrown into even more confusion. "When he left the day before yesterday, he was going to speak to you, see if you agreed we had enough evidence to bring Carter in. I haven't been able to get hold of him since then, and he hasn't answered his mobile. I'm concerned something might have happened to him."

Harper stared at Ethan. "I saw DS Stott this morning. He indicated that he still hadn't any idea where you were or even if you were alive."

Inside his chest, Ethan's heart gave a painful thump. He swallowed against a sudden wave of nausea. The windows began to mist up, adding to his sense of disorientation. What was going on?

"Sir, I don't understand. My…my cover was blown about a week ago, I managed to escape…Willow… um, I made contact with Mike several days ago." He swallowed hard, aware he wasn't giving a very coherent account of events.

Harper once again interrupted. "DS Stott told me he was working on a new lead, a female he thought might be involved in Carter's set."

"Willow." He went cold as a wave of panic swept over him. Turning on the ignition, he reached for the seatbelt. "Sir, I need to go…"

"DC McCormick." Harper's voice was calm, measured, and brooked no argument. He leaned across to switch the engine off. "I suggest you tell me what is going on."

"Sir, I can't. I have to get to Willow."

"You're going to start at the beginning, and you are not leaving here until I know exactly what the hell has been happening."

****

Sunday morning dawned bright and clear. In an attempt to lift her spirits, Willow turned the music up loud as she prepared for the Christmas Fete at the school later that morning. With Ethan taking her car, she had had to borrow the school caretaker's van to shuttle everything over to the school, and it was now crammed with boxes of handmade decorations, charms, and mince pies. The snow was melting rapidly, and she had no problems negotiating the van from her house down to the primary school at the bottom of the village.

There were still a couple of hours to go before the Fete was due to start, but the caretaker was ill and had asked if she could open up and close the school. Because she was doing him a favor, he had been more than willing to lend her the use of his van.

The carpark was deserted when she pulled into the carpark, and she quickly unlocked the main doors and set about putting on the heating. She wasn't alone for long, when just a few minutes later some of the other volunteers arrived and they began setting up their stalls in the school hall. Satisfied that everyone knew what they were doing, Willow began setting up her corner stall, having retrieved all her boxes from the van.

Carefully arranging her handmade Christmas decorations on the table, she bent down to pull the last few from her box, rummaging through the leftover bits of wrapping and tinsel.

"Oh my God!" She dropped the decorations and shot back from the table, her hands flying to her chest as she stared into the box. The gun she had taken from Ethan that first night was nestled at the bottom of the box, incongruous amongst the festive decorations.

At the next table, Helen looked at her in surprise. "Are you okay?"

Willow's head snapped around, her heart racing as she looked at Helen, who was clearly waiting for a response. Her mouth suddenly dry, she swallowed painfully. "Um…yes, yes I'm fine. Sorry, I thought I saw a huge spider at the bottom of the box, but it was just a little piece of tinsel." She forced a light laugh. "Ridiculous really. How embarrassing."

"Oh, I do that all the time." Helen waved a dismissive hand. "Brian thinks I'm a wuss, but I'm terrified of the things."

"Yes, me too," Willow said distractedly as Helen returned her attention to her own stall. She bent over the box and gingerly pushed aside the decorations to uncover the gun. How on earth had she forgotten she had hidden it in the box? She chewed her lip, looking around the room without really seeing anything clearly, wondering what to do.

She had brought a gun into a primary school, to a school fete filled with children and families. She took a deep breath, covering her mouth with her hand, and closed her eyes in an effort to think clearly. After a moment, she crouched down by the box, pulled her shoulder bag from under the table, and with a quick furtive glance to make sure no one was watching, took the gun from the box and slipped it into her bag. Zipping up the bag tightly, she slung it over her head and across her body. There. No one could get to it now.

She swallowed, dropping her hand to her stomach, trying to calm the sickening churning. Everything was fine. The gun was safe, no one would know. It was just for a couple of hours, and it was safe enough in her shoulder bag.

Trying to push thoughts of the gun to the back of her mind, she finished setting up her stall just as families started to arrive, and as the room filled with chatter and laughter and familiar people she began to relax. Yes, everything was fine.

****

It was nearing the end of the afternoon, and the rush had died down when Willow took the opportunity to wander around some of the other stalls and buy herself a cup of coffee. Seeking five minutes of peace and quiet, she made her way to her own classroom and went in, the familiar room acting like a soothing balm. She walked over to the window overlooking the little inner courtyard garden, blowing on her coffee and humming the Christmas tunes stuck in her head like an earworm after listening to the same playlist on loop all afternoon.

The garden was in a rather sorry looking state, the melting snow revealing brown, lifeless plants, but she smiled, looking forward to spring when she and the children would tidy the small garden and plant more flowers.

Unzipping her bag to pull out her phone, Willow's lips tightened when she caught sight of the gun, but she ignored it and instead checked for missed calls or messages. Nothing. Pretending she didn't feel a gut-wrenching stab of disappointment at Ethan's lack of contact, she dropped the phone back into the bag. Her glance once again fell on the gun, and after a moment she lifted it out and studied it, turning it over in her hands. According to the writing on the barrel, it was a Glock 17 Gen4. She wrinkled her nose. *Whatever that means.*

How easily could a gun accidentally go off in her bag, she wondered.

Now the thought had entered her head, she couldn't get rid of it, and, with a quick glance at her watch, she reached for her phone again. She logged onto the internet, tapping the make and model of the gun into the search engine.

Thank goodness for the school wifi.

There were pages and pages of links relating to Glocks and, after perusing several, she found one website that gave a clear overview of the gun.

To her relief, it appeared there were several safety features, which meant it was highly unlikely the gun would discharge by accident. Still, she remained uneasy and searched for instructions on how to disarm the gun. Again, several pages of links, and one in particular with clear step by step instructions.

Willow took a deep breath and seated herself at her own desk at the front of the classroom. With a wary glance toward the door, she set her phone down on the desk so she was able to use both hands to disarm the Glock and still read the instructions.

Keeping her fingers well clear of the trigger, she pointed the gun toward the back of the classroom and pressed the magazine release on the side of the gun with her thumb. With her other hand, she was able to pull the magazine out easily and place it on the desk. After a quick double check with the instructions on her phone, she pulled back the sliding barrel and locked it open by pushing up the stop lever before lifting the gun up to look into the chamber to check it was clear. She saw immediately that there were no bullets in the chamber.

Putting the gun down on the desk, she once more picked up the magazine and with her thumb pushed the top bullet forward so it fell onto the desk. The spring-loaded magazine immediately pushed up the next bullet, and she continued removing them until the magazine was empty. After double checking the gun chamber was empty, she released the sliding barrel back into place and reinserted the magazine.

The gun was now safe, and she was both relieved and proud of herself. Despite having never handled a firearm before, it had been fairly simple to disarm the Glock, and she returned it to her bag feeling much happier. Scooping the bullets from the desk, she dropped them into the zipped inside pocket in her bag. Job done.

Two hours later, Willow heaved a sigh of relief. It had been a long day, but everyone had appeared to have fun, and they had raised a reasonable amount for the school charity. Most of the stall holders had stayed behind to help her clear everything away, but now she was alone and just needed to give the school one final sweep to make sure it was clean, tidy, and, most importantly, empty before she locked up.

Placing the last of her boxes on the reception desk by the school entrance along with her keys, she began retracing her steps to do the final sweep. The school was laid out in a P shape, with the entrance hall and reception desk at the bottom of the long straight corridor. Willow turned right along the shorter corridor, systematically checking to ensure all the classrooms were empty and no one was in the bathrooms or cupboards.

Walking into her own classroom to double check she hadn't left anything in there, she paused, the warm familiarity of the room drawing her in. Without really thinking, she sank into the chair behind her desk and closed her eyes. It was so quiet, so still, and she took a moment to just *be*. Since Ethan had walked out of her life, she hadn't allowed herself to stop and think, and now she felt the weight of his leaving as a physical constriction in her chest. The huge, wracking sob took her by surprise. She lifted her gaze to the ceiling. Was that really it? Was she never going to see him again?

Willow genuinely believed everything happened for a reason, had been sure she had been in exactly the right place at the right time when Ethan climbed into her car that night. But surely this wasn't the end? He wasn't just going to walk out of her life now? It didn't make any sense. Anger and disbelief gave her a momentary relief from her pain, and she allowed it to wash over her. It felt good to be angry.

But she was fooling herself, and she knew it.

Taking a deep breath, she opened her eyes. The reason she had found herself outside that warehouse and the stars had aligned in just that way had been to ensure Ethan escaped. It hadn't been his time to die that night, thank God. For that she would be forever grateful.

And the reason for Ethan coming into her life?

She knew it had been to open her eyes to Sam. No one else could have persuaded her of what he was capable, only Ethan. Everything happened for a reason. And now it was done.

Her chin wobbled as she acknowledged the truth, and she sniffed, brushing her hair back behind her ears as she attempted to compose herself. It was almost a relief when she heard her phone buzzing in her bag, and she fumbled to answer it before it stopped. It was an unknown number, and she hesitated before answering, hoping it wasn't a call center about to ask her if she had recently had an accident.

"Hello?"

"Willow. Are you alright?"

Ethan. Her heart skipped a beat, briefly wondering if she was simply imagining his voice. She closed her eyes and took a deep, steadying breath before responding. "Yes, I'm fine, thank you." She belatedly recognized the tension in his voice. "Are you?"

"I don't know. Something's not right. Something's off." His words were clipped. "It's Mike. I haven't been able to get hold of him but, according to the DCI, he's…I think he's on his way to see you. He's still got this crazy idea you're mixed up in all of this."

She frowned as she walked over to the window overlooking the internal courtyard garden. "And…do you think that too?"

"No, of course not, but there's something not right about all this. I think he's on his way to bring you in."

"Bring me in?" She absently twisted a strand of hair around her finger. "Should I be worried?"

"I don't know what he's thinking or what evidence he thinks he's got." There was a pause, and Willow realized he was driving when she heard the blaring of a car horn, followed by an explicit curse. "Sorry about that. Look, I'm on my way to you. I don't know where Mike is or what he's doing, but I've tried to call him. If he gets to you first, just stay put until I get there. I'm only twenty minutes away now."

"Okay. Well, I've just finished up at the school fete. Doing one last check everyone's gone, and then I'm going home."

Ethan paused again. "Might not be a bad idea for you to stay there. I can meet you at the school."

"Okay, that's fine. I—"

Movement on the opposite side of the courtyard made her start in surprise.

A figure in a black hoodie slowly walked along the corridor before stopping directly opposite and turning to face her. He stood unmoving, his face invisible beneath the hood.

Fear flooded through her, preventing her from drawing breath. Her legs trembled, threatening to collapse beneath her, and a whimper escaped her lips as she struggled to breathe.

"Willow? Willow, are you there?" Ethan's voice buzzed in her ear, and she shook her head as if to negate what she was seeing.

"He's…he's here." Her voice cracked as she spoke.

"Who? Mike?"

"No. The man from the other night. In the hoodie. He's here. In the…in the school."

"He's what?" Ethan's voice snapped in her ear. "Are you sure?"

"I can see him," she whispered, blinking against the tears blurring her vision, terrified she wouldn't see him if he moved. "He's just standing there, watching me."

She heard Ethan's breathing quicken, but when he spoke his voice was calm. "Is it Sam?"

She shook her head. "It's not him. I know it isn't."

The man slowly raised his right arm. He was holding a large knife.

"Oh my God." Her voice was little more than a whisper. "Ethan, he's got a knife."

Still the same calm, low voice. "Can you get out of the school?

"Willow?" His voice was sharp when she didn't answer. "Listen to me. Can you get out of the school?"

She stared at the figure opposite, flinching when he took a step closer to the window, deliberately angling the knife to catch the light. "I don't know. Um, I think so. I'm closer to the entrance than he is."

"Then run. Get out and run to the first person you see. Now!"

His terse order jarred her into action, and she backed away from the window, her steps slow and jerky. She bumped into one of the desks, giving a cry of surprise, and was forced to look away from the figure in black as she fled to the classroom door. Flinging it open, she gave a fearful glance over her shoulder, fully expecting the corridor opposite to be empty, but he was still there. He hadn't moved, was still watching her.

Backing through the door, her eyes fixed on the stalker, she turned and ran toward the entrance hall. Panic lent speed to her feet. As she came out into the main corridor, a quick, terrified glance to her right showed a long, empty corridor with no sign of the intruder.

Quickly crossing the open space of the entrance hall, she crashed into the main doors, but her sob of relief instantly turned to despair. They wouldn't open.

Willow shook the doors in disbelief, stealing glances over her shoulder to make sure he wasn't behind her, but the doors were locked. Keys. She'd left her keys on the reception hatch.

A single step toward the hatch confirmed her keys weren't there. How could that be? She'd left them by the boxes, and now there was simply an empty space.

Her knees buckled as she fought against the dizziness dimming her vision. With trembling fingers, she lifted the phone to her ear. Ethan was still driving, waiting for her to tell him she was safe. Her voice broke as she spun around, searching for a way to escape. "He's taken my keys. I'm locked in."

"Okay, listen to me." His voice was quiet and firm. "You know the school inside out. He doesn't. You're going to find somewhere to hide until I get there. Okay? Willow, are you listening to me? You need to hide."

"Okay. Yes. I'll hide." Her breath came in short, sharp gasps. She was beginning to hyperventilate.

"It's going to be okay. I'm not far away now, but you need to calm your breathing down. I can hear you, and he's going to be able to hear you too. Long, deep breaths."

Slow, heavy footsteps echoed along the long corridor, and Willow's breath stilled in her throat. "Ethan. He's coming!"

"Hide, Willow. I'm on my way."

Chapter Sixteen

It was a dark afternoon, but the lights and the Christmas decorations in the school made for a cheerful entrance hall. It sat at odds with the fear that kept Willow frozen to the spot. She wasted valuable seconds looking around frantically without really seeing anything, but as the footsteps got louder, they galvanized her into action. She sprinted toward the short corridor.

Seeking the first place she could find, she ran into the reception office and crouched down in the space between the wall and the desk. It hid her from view from both the reception hatch and the small window in the door.

The slow, heavy footsteps drew nearer as he approached the entrance hall, and Willow pressed her spine closer against the wall, wishing herself invisible. A buzzing sound made her blink in fear, before realizing it was coming from the phone in her hand. Ethan was still talking.

She switched it off, terrified her stalker would hear. She was on her own now. If he opened the door and came in, he would see her immediately. She willed him to move away, but the footsteps paused outside in the entrance hall, and she imagined him slowly turning around, searching for her.

"Wil-low."

She jumped at the sudden sound of his voice. The long, drawn out use of her name and the eerie tone of his voice caused a shiver to run down her spine. He was close. His voice was just above her head, and she shrank back against the wall, holding her breath. Now he was leaning in through the reception hatch.

Please, don't let him hear me breathing.

She heard him give a muffled curse, and then his footsteps receded down the corridor once more. In danger of becoming paralyzed by fear, she needed to find somewhere safer to hide until Ethan arrived, but where?

Think, Willow, think.

Opening her eyes, her gaze fell upon a row of switches on the wall opposite. That panel controlled the lighting for the whole school. If she could switch off the lights, she would have an advantage over the stalker. He wasn't familiar with the layout of the school, she was. It wasn't much of an advantage, but it was something.

Willow stared at the panel on the wall, willing herself to move. She was running out of time before he came back and took a closer look at the room she was in. But part of her wanted nothing more than to stay here in her little corner, even though it wasn't safe.

Move!

Fighting against the debilitating fear, she inched from her hiding place. With a wary glance over her shoulder through the reception hatch, she reached a trembling hand for the panel of switches.

About to turn the main key, she hesitated as a thought crossed her mind. She had known where the stranger was because she could hear his footsteps, could hear the heavy boots he was obviously wearing. She looked down at her own boots and, after a moment, pulled them off and shoved them under the desk. She stood very still, listening for any sound that might tell her he was near.

After a moment she heard him calling her name. He didn't sound close.

This was probably her best shot. The moment she turned off the lights, she imagined him running down to the entrance hall, and she needed to be gone when he got here. But which way would he turn? The biggest risk was running straight into him.

Willow closed her eyes. She willed her heartbeat to slow, to stop the deafening, non-stop thudding in her ears, and blew out a long, slow breath. Lifting her hand to grasp the key on the wall panel, she firmly turned it to the left. The building was instantly plunged into semi-darkness. Running to the door, she opened it quietly and eased herself out into the corridor. She listened, poised for flight, and again closed her eyes to concentrate on determining where he was.

A long, low laugh echoed down the corridor; clearly, he was still some distance away. "Are we playing a game, Willow?"

She opened her eyes. He was at the top of the long corridor; she was almost certain. If she took two steps to her left, she would step out into that corridor and be able to look down to the end, but it was too risky. If he was there, he would see her immediately.

The next moment she heard him walking quickly down the corridor and nearly leaped out of her skin. Turning to her right, she sprinted down the short corridor, away from him, her footsteps silent in her thick woolen socks. Following the corridor around to her left, her breath came in short, harsh gasps as she fled toward the school hall. Entering the hall, she skidded to a halt, almost falling as her socks slipped on the shiny, vinyl flooring.

"Wil-low." His voice echoed from the corridor at the opposite side of the room; he must have doubled back. He knew she was running from him. "Come out, come out, wherever you are."

The hall was similar to most primary schools—a multi-use space that facilitated morning assembly, dining hall, and PE. Folding climbing apparatus was pushed back against two walls, with the third wall having a deep recess. It was curtained off from the hall and acted as a storeroom for the smaller pieces of PE equipment. It was, in fact, quite a large space, almost another room, and Willow ran quickly across the hall.

She knew the storeroom had an odd lip to one side of the entrance, creating a narrow recess hidden from view. It had probably originally been intended to enclose pipes or electrical wiring but had never been used or sealed off. Whatever, it was now an anomaly, a hidden space no one would see unless they knew it was there.

As she ducked behind the curtain, her gaze fell on the wooden gym horse, and she briefly considered hiding inside but shuddered to think she might be trapped within its hollow, claustrophobic confines. Instead, she turned to the tower of boxes to her left, piled on top of one another, seemingly flush against the wall. She nodded. He would never guess there was a gap behind that section of wall.

She crouched down to pull the bottom box forward a little. It was awkward, but the boxes were only filled with plastic balls and spare gym kit, so it wasn't too heavy. She only needed to pull it enough for her to squeeze behind. The boxes made a scraping sound as they moved, appearing loud in the absolute silence, and she prayed he wasn't yet close enough to hear. Giving the boxes one last tug, she straightened up. It would have to do.

"Wil-low. I'm going to find you." The sing-song voice grew louder, and she quickly squeezed down by the side of the boxes, biting her lip as her shoulder bag caught on the edge.

He was in the hall.

She reached the back of the tower of boxes and shuffled down the other side into the hidden recess, fighting to control her breathing, knowing it was too loud.

"I'm liking this little game, Willow." His slow, heavy footsteps echoed around the hall. "Creates anticipation. Gives me time to think about what I'm going to do to you when I find you."

She hugged her bag to her chest and squeezed her eyes shut. How long until Ethan arrived?

The sound of the curtain being drawn back snapped her eyes open wide. She held her breath.

"Are you in here, Willow?" The soft voice was so close, just a few inches of plaster separated them.

She choked back a sob. Her legs were shaking so badly she was only able to stay upright because of the enclosed space she was squeezed into.

The next moment, there was a deafening bang, frightening the life out of her, and she clapped her hands over her mouth to prevent the scream escaping her lips. A further bang, and the sound of something falling over, followed by a string of curses. She guessed he had kicked over the gym horse to see if she was hiding inside.

"Where the fuck are you, you bitch?"

His footsteps receded, and she sagged back against the wall, her knees bending slightly in the narrow space. Silent, terrified sobs wracked her body as she pressed her fingers against her mouth.

Please, Ethan. Hurry.

She would have slid to the floor, but the recess was so narrow that as her knees weakened she ended up in an odd half sitting position, knees jammed against the wall in front. She was relatively safe for the moment, but it was only a matter of time before he searched the rooms more thoroughly.

What about Ethan? He wasn't safe either. She'd brought him into danger too. She tried to reassure herself that Ethan knew what he was doing. This was his job, and he could take care of himself. Besides, he was probably the best chance she had of getting out.

The sudden sound of a mobile phone ringing almost caused her to cry out in surprise, and she froze for a moment thinking it was hers. But then she realized it came from somewhere out in the hall.

He was back.

"Ethan, what's happening? Where are you?"

Willow's eyes snapped open. *Did he just say Ethan?*

"The school? That's where I am; someone in the village told me Willow was here. Wait, wait, slow down…" There was a pause. "No. No, the doors were unlocked, I've done a sweep of the building, and there's no one here. Where are you anyway? I thought we agreed you were going to stay here with her…? Okay, okay…no, there's no intruder. Mate, are you sure she was in trouble?"

Willow straightened up slowly, staring at the wall just inches from her nose in the semi-darkness. Was that Mike? Relief flooded through her. She wasn't alone. He may think she was somehow mixed up in Carter's gang, but he wouldn't see her come to any harm. She bit her lip. But where was the intruder?

"Okay, look, I gotta say it, Ethan, you know I don't believe in this hoodie guy. There's no sign anything untoward happened here, no struggle, the doors were unlocked. Nothing." He was closer now. Again, a long pause, and then a heavy sigh. "Okay, I'll do another search. If she's hiding, I'll find her. How long until you get here? Okay, I'll see you in five."

There were a few moments of silence. Willow was just about to call out to Mike when she heard a long, low laugh. A laugh that sent a shiver of ice along her spine.

"Wil-low. Not long to wait now," he called out in a sing-song voice. "Your boyfriend's coming, and then we can really have some fun."

Willow pressed her fist into her mouth, biting down on her knuckles to prevent the wail building inside her from escaping.

It was Mike. Mike was the stalker in the hoodie.

She began to shake. Darkness pressed in on the edges of her vision. She sagged against the wall, her chest constricting, tightening like a band until it was difficult to draw breath. She shook her head, palms flat against the wall in front of her. She was having a panic attack.

Breathe. Come on Willow, breathe. Slowly.

She sucked in a long, slow breath, fighting the urge to gasp in as much air as possible, and then forced herself to blow out again slowly. After what seemed like an age, she no longer felt as if she was having a heart attack and was able to breathe normally. It didn't stop the tremors wracking her body but at least she was able to breathe.

Ethan.

He was walking into a trap. Mike had to be the insider. God, Ethan had no idea.

She fumbled in her bag for her phone, and brought it up to her face, squinting in pain at the brightness of the screen in the dim, narrow confines of her hiding place.

No signal.

Willow bit back a scream, looking up at the ceiling in fear and frustration. She had to do something.

****

The car slewed from side to side as Ethan drove into the school carpark too fast and braked too hard on the snow. Hardly caring that he narrowly missed the van parked nearest the entrance, he cut the engine and jumped out of the car. He sprinted toward the doors, praying he wasn't too late and that Mike had found Willow before the stranger had.

Mike was waiting for him as he rushed through the doors. He held up his hands to slow Ethan's headlong flight. "Whoa, whoa, slow down."

"Where is she? Have you found her?" He was gasping for breath, more from fear than from physical exertion. It seemed like hours since she'd hung up on him, although he knew it was only fifteen, twenty minutes at the most.

The heavy feeling in the pit of his stomach told him he was too late; he'd failed her. He squeezed his eyes shut, trying to push away the negative thoughts that threatened to paralyze him. If she was still here, still hiding, she needed him to think clearly.

Mike shook his head. "She's not here, mate. I've looked everywhere."

Ethan spun away from him in frustration. He pulled out his phone and dialed her number. It went straight to voicemail.

"Dammit, she can't have any signal." He turned back to Mike. "She's got to be here. I don't know, hiding somewhere."

Mike leveled a long stare at him before nodding slowly. "Okay, let's sweep the place again." He grasped Ethan's shoulder. "If she's here, we'll find her."

Ethan nodded and turned to stride down the shorter corridor to the right. He flicked a sideways glance at Mike as he hurried to catch up. "Want to tell me why you haven't taken my calls? Why you told Harper you haven't heard from me in weeks?"

Mike didn't answer immediately. He pushed open the door to the reception office, stepped in, and looked around. It was clearly empty, and he retreated from the room, but Ethan's hand on his arm stopped him. He pointed to the control panel for the lights and reached across to turn the key. Light once more flooded the building.

Mike grinned. "Not just a pretty face, are you?"

Ethan didn't smile back. "Well?"

His partner sighed as they resumed their search of the building, walking along the short corridor and checking the classroom doors as they passed. They were all locked.

“Okay, I didn’t tell Harper because, like you, I didn’t know who the insider was.” He held up his hand as Ethan started to respond. “And because I needed time. Your girl is in on this, Ethan, right up to her neck, and I’m going find out just how deep.”

“Mike, I swear to God…” Ethan struggled to contain his fear and anger. He stopped and turned to face his partner as they drew into the hall. “And that stunt with the mobile phone? I ought to punch your lights out for that right now.”

He pulled the phone from his pocket and held it up with an accusing look at his partner. Mike had the good grace to look uncomfortable, and he took the phone from Ethan. “I needed something to try and knock some sense into you. She’s got you tied up in knots.”

Ethan narrowed his eyes. “No. There’s something not right here, and I need you to tell me what the hell is going on.”

Mike dropped his head and gave a defeated sigh before looking back up at Ethan. He gave a half smile. “Okay, you’re right. Look, I—” His gaze shifted to focus on something over Ethan’s shoulder, and his expression changed to one of surprise. “Willow!”

Ethan spun around, relief flooding through him, but the hall behind him was empty. The next moment he felt a sharp pain across the back of his head and then… nothing.

****

Willow shuffled backward out of the recess when she heard voices and stilled. Standing behind the wall of boxes, listening intently, she realized it wasn't quite as dimly lit as before. There was a band of light along the top and bottom of the curtain; Mike had turned the lights back on. The voices grew louder as they reached the hall.

"No. There's something not right here, and I need you to tell me what the hell is going on."

"Okay, you're right. Look, I…Willow!"

The relief on hearing Ethan's voice was cut short when she heard Mike call her name. Fear flooded through her, had he seen her somehow? She stared in horror at the curtain, expecting it to be whipped across at any moment, but instead she heard a thud, a sharp cry, and then the sound of something hitting the floor.

"Too bad, Ethan. You just got too close."

Willow blinked in shock, nausea welling up at the back of her throat, knees suddenly weak. What had Mike done? She had to see. Without thinking, she moved quickly along the boxes, wincing as her skirt brushed against them, but the sound of Mike dragging something along the floor covered any sounds she might be making.

What was he dragging?

Ethan. It could only be Ethan. She shook her head, chasing away that paralyzing thought. Moving free of the boxes, she pressed herself flat against the wall. She needed to move closer to the edge of the curtain to see what was happening in the hall. Mike was muttering something to himself, but there was no sound from Ethan.

She lifted a trembling hand to her lips, squeezing her eyes shut as she attempted to slow her heart rate and her breathing. She forced herself to inch closer until she stood at the edge of the recess, her spine still pressed flat against the wall.

Gathering her courage, she leaned to the side and carefully peered through the centimeter gap between the edge of the curtain and the wall. The thin sliver of hall she was able to see was empty.

A strange, metallic sound made her jump, and she only just managed to swallow the cry of surprise that would have given away her hiding place. She took a few more steadying breaths, then pushed herself from the wall. Moving quickly across the curtain to the other side of the recess, she resumed her stance against the wall and leaned to look through the gap. Her heart gave one painful thump against her chest, and she was unable to breathe when she saw Ethan. He appeared unconscious, sitting on the floor and propped up against the PE apparatus on the wall. His wrists were handcuffed to the metal bars above his head. Blood was oozing from a cut on his left temple, but as she watched she saw him stir and groan. His eyelids fluttered open to focus on the figure of his friend and partner crouching in front of him.

"Mike?" His voice was weak and confused.

"Good. I'm glad you're awake. Let's just get things moving, shall we?" Mike's voice was cold as he stood.

As he turned toward Willow's hiding place, she shrank back against the wall, even though logic told her he wouldn't be able to see her.

"Oh Wil-low, your boyfriend's here," he called, his voice bouncing weirdly off the walls as he turned in a circle. "Time to come out and play."

"Willow!"

She jumped at the sound of Ethan's voice, now stronger as he shouted for her, and she leaned once more to peer through the curtain.

"Willow. The doors are open. Run, just run—"

Mike threw a vicious punch, and Willow bit back a scream as his fist connected with Ethan's jaw. His head snapped to the side, blood flying from his split lip. From her vantage point, she saw him slowly turn to look back at Mike, and a shiver ran through her at the deadly venom she saw in his gaze when he looked at his partner.

Mike once more crouched at Ethan's side, his back to Willow, as he called out again.

"You better hurry up, Willow. Every minute you stay hidden, I'm going to carve up your pretty boy." He waited a few seconds, his head on one side as if listening. "No? Not coming out to play? Fair enough."

She stared, frozen in horror, as he slowly withdrew the knife from the back waistband of his jeans and casually unbuttoned Ethan's shirt. Ethan let loose a stream of vicious curses, pulling ineffectually at the handcuffs above his head, and kicking out at Mike, who simply cuffed him across the side of his head with the butt of the knife, leaving him stunned.

"You mentioned a little scratch, my friend," said Mike quietly, as Willow strained to hear him. "Let's have a little look-see, shall we?"

Ethan shook his head, still dazed, and didn't react when Mike removed the dressing from his side. He gave a low whistle. "Mate, that was some scratch. Looks like it's healing pretty well, though." He laughed. "Let's see what we can do about that."

Unable to tear her gaze away, Willow watched in horror as Mike slowly and surely drew the knife down along the row of neat stitches. Ethan screamed as the blade slipped easily into the wound and reopened it.

She spun away from the curtain, dropping to her knees, mouth open in a silent scream alongside Ethan's. She squeezed her eyes shut, retching painfully, unable to rid herself of the image of Mike cutting Ethan open.

"You…bastard," Ethan managed. "I'll kill you."

"That's why I've got you in handcuffs, my friend."

She sat back on her heels, swallowing hard against nausea, allowing red-hot anger to rise in its place. Dashing away her tears with the back of her hand, she got to her feet. She wasn't going to let Mike hurt Ethan anymore.

Scrabbling in her bag, still slung across her shoulder, she found her mobile phone. Still no signal, but as she dropped it back in the bag her eyes settled on the gun. She cursed herself for emptying it earlier. Could she reload it? Did she have enough time?

"Now then, shall we see if we can get something similar on the other side, Ethan?" Mike raised his voice. "Did you hear that, Willow? I can make him scream louder if you want me to. You've got one minute before I carve your boyfriend into shreds."

She looked around frantically, searching for something, anything. Her gaze fell on a box in the corner. "Rounders bats" was written on the side in big black letters. An idea formed in her mind as she stared at it, shaking her head as Mike shouted that she had thirty seconds left.

Without stopping to think any further, knowing she risked losing her nerve if she did, she ran to the box. Carefully pulling out a bat, she hefted it in her hand. The old-fashioned solid wood was reassuringly heavy.

She reached behind her to tuck the bat in the waistband of her skirt so it lay flat along her spine underneath her coat. Taking the gun from her bag, she turned to the curtain, taking deep breaths to control her fear, drawing on her anger.

A swift look through the gap in the curtain confirmed Mike still had his back to her. He was blocking her view of Ethan. With a shaking hand, she pulled the curtain aside and slipped through. Not really sure why she didn't want Mike to know where she had been hiding, she swiftly side-stepped along the wall to the corridor.

She brought the gun up to point at Mike as he caught sight of her in his peripheral vision and turned toward her. For a second, his jaw dropped, and his eyes widened in surprise at the sight of her standing there, pointing a gun at him, and then he relaxed into a delighted laugh.

"Hoo-eee! Well, look at you there, going all Lara fucking Croft on me." He turned to Ethan, slumped against the apparatus. "I'm beginning to see why you like this girl."

Ethan looked up, his own eyes widening when he saw her. He immediately straightened, pulling frantically at the handcuffs pinning his hands above his head. "Willow, for God's sake! What are you doing? Just get out of here."

"Let him go, Mike." She took a step forward, trying desperately to stop her hand from shaking as she continued to hold the gun straight out in front of her.

"Well, you've got some balls, honey," he said, looking down at the floor with a grin. "Is that thing even loaded?"

She fought to keep her face expressionless.

He couldn't know, could he? Could you tell if a gun was empty just by looking?

She lifted her chin, her gaze fixed on Mike's. "Ethan, this is the gun you had that night. Was it loaded when you were waving it around at me?"

"Willow, please…"

"Was it loaded?" she repeated through gritted teeth.

"Yes."

She managed a shrug. "Well, then I guess it's loaded."

Chapter Seventeen

Mike's grin widened as he casually tucked the knife in the back waistband of his jeans. He took a step forward, his grin fading to be replaced by a cold menace. Willow was hit by a wave of black energy as it radiated from him, making her flinch. "You point a gun at me, you bitch, you better be prepared to use it."

He took another step toward her, then another. She fought to stand her ground but was unable to stop the gun from wavering as her hand shook with terror. She dashed a hand across her eyes to brush away the tears blurring her vision.

"Mike, you bastard…" Ethan struggled against the handcuffs. "You hurt her, and you'll wish to God you were never born."

Mike ignored him. He now stood in front of Willow, and with one final step he moved close enough for the gun to touch his chest. Neither one moved for several tense moments. Her knees trembled beneath her long skirt as she fought to return his gaze.

Mike suddenly flashed out a hand to snatch the gun from her, his other hand grabbing a handful of her hair. Before she knew what was happening, he was dragging her across the room toward Ethan. He thrust the gun under her chin, and she cried out, closing her eyes as she waited for him to pull the trigger and realize the gun was empty.

“No!” Ethan yelled.

“Well, here we all are,” said Mike softly, his lips close to Willow’s ear. Her eyes snapped open at the sound of his voice so close. His fingers tightened in her hair, and she gasped in pain, more tears springing to her eyes. It felt as if he was ripping her hair out by the roots. “So, how are we going to do this?”

Her gaze sought Ethan. He was deathly pale with beads of sweat peppering his forehead, mixing with the blood, but his gaze was alert and watchful. A pulse throbbed in his jaw, and as he shifted his weight he winced. Her eyes dropped to his side, and her stomach lurched when she saw the blood oozing from his wound. As her own senses cleared, she smelled the coppery scent of blood on the air.

“Mike.” Ethan’s voice was clipped but even. “I don’t know what this is about, but Willow isn’t anything to do with it. This is about you and me. She’s not important. Just let her go.”

She’s not important.

His words hit Willow hard, and she closed her eyes briefly at the pain they caused. She knew he was only saying it to persuade Mike to let her go, but still, they hurt.

“Not important?” Mike’s fingers tightened once more, and as he shook her Willow clamped her mouth shut to prevent the cry of pain escaping her lips. She wouldn’t give him the satisfaction. “Well, see, that’s what I thought too. Until I saw the two of you the other night in the pub. She’s clearly very important to you. Look at you; she’s made you weak.”

“I don’t get it.” Ethan seemed intent on keeping the conversation going. “What is this about? I take it you’re the insider, and the guy in the hoodie too. You blew my cover. Why?"

"Money," said Mike casually, after a moment. "That thing that makes the world go around. I could stand here and spill my guts to you, Ethan, tell you all about my gambling debts, the blackmail, the threats…and then the little bits of information I handed to Carter to pay off those debts. It's actually a long, sorry story, mate, but at the end of it we'd still be here, with you getting too close to the truth for your own good."

The burning pain across Willow's scalp receded a little when Mike's fingers relaxed and his shoulders slumped.

"You should have listened, mate," he said quietly. "I told you not to take that job, tried to warn you off, but you wouldn't listen. And now, here we are."

"Mike, we can work this out. You know we can." Ethan blinked and hissed as blood ran into his eye. "Just let Willow go, and we can talk."

"I'm afraid not. You see, Willow here is key to my plan." Mike straightened, his voice hardening once more. "And you know what? She continues to play a blinder, making it easy for me. Here she is, bringing me a gun, one of Carter's guns, the gun I'm going to use to kill you, and which is covered in her fingerprints."

He held up his gloved hand, holding the gun. "I'm afraid I got here too late to save you, Ethan. I tried to warn you she was part of Carter's gang, but you wouldn't listen, and that cost you your life. But you'll be glad to know I survived after killing this bitch here in self-defense, of course."

"Oh, just one more thing," he said, with a pleasant smile, glancing between the two of them. He slipped the gun into his jacket pocket before reaching around to his back and withdrawing the knife.

Willow's stomach lurched; the chances of her plan working were fading fast. She needed the element of surprise the empty gun would give her. It had always been a slim chance, but a chance, nonetheless.

Mike released her hair to grasp her wrist, pressing the knife into her palm, and using his own hand to force her fingers around the handle. Seemingly satisfied, he took the knife from her once more and carefully slipped it back into the waistband of his jeans. "That'll do."

She gasped when he resumed his grip on her hair, his gaze fixed on Ethan. "Well, I think we're done talking. You're probably getting close to bleeding out, my friend, and I'd much prefer to make you suffer before you pass out."

Mike pulled Willow close. Taking the gun from his pocket to press the muzzle against her temple, he kissed her. His tongue forced its way through her lips, and she struggled against him, heard Ethan shouting, fighting against the cuffs that held him captive. Mike flinched as Ethan's foot connected with the back of his knee, and he dragged his mouth from hers. Spittle clung to her lip for a few nauseating seconds, and she shrank from his foul breath, as if the dark energy he radiated emanated from within him.

"You're going to regret that," he growled at Ethan.

He slid his hand to the back of her neck, releasing her hair with a suddenness that made her stumble. He pushed her with him as he stood over Ethan. Lifting the gun, he pointed it toward his partner.

Willow began to tremble. This was it. Luck had swung back in her favor. She needed to be close enough to Mike when he realized the gun wasn't loaded to be able to carry out her plan.

Mike slowly raised the gun and placed it against Ethan's forehead.

Ethan didn't flinch, and his gaze didn't waver from Mike's. His eyes were filled with hatred. He pressed his head forward against the gun. "Do it, you bastard."

"Oh, I will. But not just yet. I want you alive for now, Ethan, so you enjoy the fun I'm going to have with your girl here." He grinned. "It doesn't mean we can't inflict a bit of pain though, does it?"

He lowered the gun to Ethan's knee, turning his head to look at Willow. "I can feel you trembling." He closed his eyes and smiled, taking a deep breath. "I like that. I'm going to enjoy making you tremble even more."

As he turned back to Ethan, Willow slowly and carefully slid her arm beneath her coat, feeling for the rounders bat pressed against her spine. She fought to control her breathing as her fingers closed around the solid wood.

Mike pulled the trigger.

Despite the anti-climactic click of the hammer hitting the empty gun chamber, it made her jump. Taking advantage of Mike's momentary confusion, she pulled the bat from her waistband. He was looking at the gun, and she saw the moment he realized what had happened. As he turned, she drove the head of the rounders bat into his stomach as hard as she could.

Mike immediately doubled over with a grunt of surprise and pain, and she brought the bat down hard across the back of his shoulders. He dropped to his knees, the useless gun flying from his hand and skittering across the floor as he struggled to draw breath.

Frozen in shock at what she had just done, Willow looked up to see Ethan's fingers curl around the bar above his head, taking his weight. A split second later he caught Mike, on his knees in front of him, in a headlock between his legs, twisting to pull his partner off balance.

Unable to breathe, his windpipe pressed against Ethan's knee, Mike's hands clawed at Ethan, an odd keening sound coming from his throat as his face turned purple. Grunting with the effort it was costing him, Ethan grimaced as he continued to squeeze the breath from his partner. Mike's movements slowed until eventually he collapsed face down onto the floor, and Ethan pushed him away with his foot.

For a few seconds there was nothing but stunned silence as Mike lay motionless, and then Willow took a few hesitant steps backward. The rounders bat fell from her fingers as the enormity of what had just happened hit her. She brought her hands up to her ears, shaking her head.

"Oh my God, what have we done? Is he dead?"

"Willow, it's okay, it's okay."

She hardly registered Ethan's calm voice, unable to take her eyes from the prone body on the floor.

"Willow, look at me."

She flinched at his sharp voice and dragged her gaze from Mike to Ethan. Her eyes filled with tears when she met his gaze. He would make everything all right.

"I need you to get the knife and the key for these cuffs," he said calmly, carefully. "They're in his jacket pocket. I need to you get them for me."

She immediately began backing away again, shaking her head. “No, no, I can’t. I can’t.”

“Yes, you can. He’s unconscious, he can’t hurt you. But we need to get the knife, and I need to get out of these cuffs before he comes around.” He gave her an encouraging smile. “Come on, Willow, you can do this. You just saved my life. You can do this.”

He nodded his head as she looked at him. He was right, she could do this. Lifting her chin, she moved slowly toward Mike, crouched down next to him, and reached out a hand, trying to ignore the fact it was shaking.

With her gaze fixed on Mike’s face, she slipped her hand into his jacket pocket. It was empty. She gave a whimper and snatched her hand back, expecting his eyes to open at any moment.

“It’s okay. Check the other pocket.”

Breathing steadily out through her mouth, she checked his other pocket. Relief flooded through her as her fingers closed around the small key, and she stood, stepping away from him hastily. “I’ve got them.”

Ethan closed his eyes in relief, his head sagging forward for a moment before looking back up at her. “Great. You’re doing really well. Now, you need to get the knife. It’s underneath his jacket.”

It was as if an invisible hook was caught in the back of her coat, preventing her from moving toward Mike. Her knees shook with the effort it took to remain standing. Nevertheless, she inched her way toward him and lifted the back of his jacket. The sight of the wicked looking knife tucked in his jeans made her wince, but she reached forward and removed it. The blade was smeared with blood. Ethan’s blood.

"That's great, Willow. Now, I need the key to unlock these cuffs."

She nodded, and hurried over to him, heart thudding in her chest. The front of his shirt was sodden with his blood, and it stuck to his torso. More blood stained his jeans and pooled on the floor beside him. She'd never seen so much blood. Her vision swam, and she blinked away the dizziness threatening to disable her. She had to stay focused; Ethan needed her.

Swallowing hard, she dropped the knife behind the bench, glad to be rid of the hateful thing, and turned her attention to the handcuffs. Her fingers were shaking so badly she couldn't get the key in the lock, and she gave a frustrated sob.

"It's okay. Take your time."

At last, the key slid into the lock, and she turned it to release the cuffs. With a groan of relief, Ethan slipped his hands from the cuffs and dropped his arms, his groan lengthening as his shoulder muscles complained at the sudden movement. Willow dropped to her knees beside him and slid her arms around his neck, burying her face against his shoulder, sobbing with relief that it was all over.

With some effort, Ethan wrapped his arms around her and kissed the top of her head. "It's okay, I've got you. I've got you." His arms slowly tightened as feeling returned to his cramped limbs. "Shhh. It's okay." He pulled away to look at her, cupping her face with his hands. "You disarmed the gun?"

When she nodded, he smiled, wincing as the movement pulled his split lip, and he shook his head. "You're amazing, Willow Daniels." His eyelids fluttered closed, and his smile faded, but after a moment he straightened up with obvious effort. “But we’re not done yet. I need to secure Mike.”

He gently unhooked her arms from around his neck. “I need to call the police and an ambulance. Can you get me a first aid kit? There must be one here in the school?” He ducked his head to look at her. “Can you do that for me?”

Willow blinked, throwing a quick glance toward Mike, and then straightened her shoulders. She nodded. “Yes, of course.”

His tense expression relaxed into a smile. “Good.”

He grasped the bars of the apparatus behind him to help him stand up, one hand pressed against his side, but still his knees threatened to give way, and he was only partially successful in biting back the cry of pain. Willow hooked an arm under his shoulders to steady him until he was able to stand.

His face was deathly pale, drawn and tense when he looked up at Willow. “Hurry.”

She nodded and ran through the school to the reception office, faltering with several keys to unlock the first aid cupboard before grabbing the kit.

By the time she got back, Ethan had managed to drag Mike close enough to the apparatus to secure his hands to the bars with the handcuffs. Ethan himself was slumped a little distance away from him, his hand clamped to his side, eyes closed, and the mobile phone on the floor beside him.

“Ethan!” Her heart skipped a beat as she hurried over, fearing he had lost consciousness, but his eyes fluttered open at the sound of her voice.

“I’m okay,” he managed a wan smile. “Just need to stop this bleeding.”

She dropped to her knees beside him and snapped open the first aid box. “I’m not sure I’ve got anything big enough to cover that wound.” She rummaged through the box without really seeing anything but stopped as Ethan’s fingers closed around her wrist.

“Hey, it’s okay,” he said, his smile a little stronger this time. “It’s going to be okay. You can do this. You’re my guardian angel. You always save me.”

She gave a relieved smile, encouraged by the fact he was still alert. She found two large sterile dressings and decided they would have to do. “This is going to hurt.”

“Go for it.” Ethan’s eyes had closed again. He hissed but didn’t flinch when she pressed the two dressings to his wound and quickly wrapped a bandage around his waist to secure the dressings.

That done and following Ethan’s instructions to wipe her fingerprints from the knife, there wasn’t a great deal else to do except wait for the police and the ambulance to arrive. She settled down next to him.

He pulled her close into his other side. “My brave, brave Willow. What did I do to deserve you?”

Chapter Eighteen

"Is Ethan okay?"

From across the table in the interview room, Detective Inspector Reyes, a slim, dark-haired woman with cold, blue eyes, and Detective Sergeant Cook, a serious-looking auburn-haired man in his thirties, simply looked at Willow without responding.

"Let's go back to the beginning, shall we?" DI Reyes appeared prepared to continue the interview all night. Willow had already told them everything she knew; after sitting in a cell for several hours, she had been taken to the interview room and subjected to question after question for over two hours. The duty solicitor had advised her to offer "no comment" to any and all questions, but Willow had opted for telling the truth, after all she had nothing to hide.

"Miss Daniels." DI Reyes appeared bored. "You surely can't expect us to believe that you, a lone female, late at night, when apprehended and held at gun point, forced to drive by an armed, supposedly dangerous assailant, would not take the opportunity to pitch him out of the car as soon as he lost consciousness? That instead, you decided to take him to your home in an extremely remote village, where you proceeded to tend to his wounds and offer him a place to stay."

Willow sighed in frustration. "I know how it sounds, but you had to be there. Like I said, I—"

"You trusted him." Sarcasm dripped from her voice as DI Reyes turned to her fellow officer. "If someone got into my car, thrust a gun in my face, and told me to drive, I can't think of many scenarios where I'd trust him, can you DS Cook?"

"He didn't feel dangerous," Willow said quietly, knowing this hard-nosed woman wasn't going to understand but needing to explain anyway. "I just get a…a sense for people. And Ethan had a good aura."

For the first time since the interview started, DI Reyes' implacable mask slipped, and she gaped at her in surprise. "A good aura?"

She nodded, lifting her chin a little in defiance.

"Well, I've heard everything now." Once again, DI Reyes turned to DS Cook, a smirk playing across her lips. "This might be a new way of catching criminals, DS Cook. Sod the profiling, the investigative legwork, and the forensics, let's just get people like Miss Daniels here to tell us if they've got a good aura."

Heat stole across Willow's cheeks, but she held DI Reyes' gaze.

"So, tell me. What does my aura say to you?" The DI's voice was laced with contempt.

She stared at the woman sitting across from her, sensed the anticipation in the room, even the bored looking duty solicitor sat up a little straighter. She couldn't help herself and pulled a face shrugging her shoulders. "I have to say, I probably wouldn't have taken you home if it had been you holding me at gunpoint that night."

DI Reyes' mouth dropped open, and from the corner of her eye Willow saw DS Cook's mouth twitch as if he were trying not to smile. She bit back her own smile, a sense of satisfaction stealing over her even as she realized she had probably not done herself any favors, judging by the stony expression on the woman's face.

Willow sighed and shook her head. "Please, why don't you just ask Ethan? He'll be able to back me up."

The fact they hadn't responded to her pleas to know how he was, that they clearly hadn't spoken to him, frightened her. The police and the ambulance had arrived less than twenty minutes after his call, but even so Ethan had drifted into unconsciousness. What if he hadn't regained consciousness? What if, God forbid, what if he was dead?

"Like I said, Miss Daniels. Let's go back to the beginning."

DS Reyes settled back in her chair as if completely prepared to stay there all night.

****

Willow turned over, pulled the covers higher over her ears, and shut her eyes, determined to go back to sleep. DI Reyes had questioned her for a full four hours last night, her manner one of disbelief. From the accusations thrown at her, Willow guessed that Mike had regained consciousness, had put forward the planted mobile as evidence, and was feeding the line of questioning. Exhausted and frightened for Ethan, she had begun to fear that despite her innocence, she was going to be charged with heaven only knew what. She didn't dare even contemplate Ethan's continued silence.

It had ended when just after midnight an officer entered the interview room and whispered something in DI Reyes' ear. With a look of intense dislike, the woman had paused the interview and left with DS Cook. Several minutes later, another officer had entered the room and told Willow she was free to leave. That was it, no explanations, no reasoning, nothing.

Exhausted, tearful, and emotional, she had signed for and collected her personal belongings from the desk sergeant. As she turned to leave, he had casually tossed her the keys to her vehicle.

"Ethan said to pass these to you. Far side of the carpark, last row."

Hope soared within her, tears of relief filling her eyes. "He's okay?"

Something in her face must have tugged at the desk sergeant's conscience because his expression softened, and he nodded. "Yes, he's going to be okay."

Lack of sleep and food, along with overwhelming relief, finally took its toll, and as her knees buckled she clutched at the duty desk to prevent herself from falling to the floor. After a moment's hesitation, the sergeant hurried around and helped her to a seat, clearly moved by her sobs of distress.

"Come on now, miss, sit here. You've been through quite an ordeal." He brought her a cup of hot coffee and retreated behind his desk, but Willow barely noticed. Ethan was going to be okay.

Ten minutes later, cold, tired, and still struggling to process the events of the last twenty-four hours, she pulled her jacket closer as she walked across to her car. The wing mirror had been fixed, she noted as she slid into the driver's seat. It was well below freezing, and she shivered, quickly closing the door and turning on the engine. Turning up the dial as high as it would go, she waited for the cold air to turn warm, staring absently at the misted-up windscreen, in no particular hurry to go anywhere.

The screen finally cleared, and the air blown out by the heater meant she was comfortably warm when she managed to rouse herself enough to fasten her seatbelt and put the car in gear. She didn't remember the journey home, only that a lump had formed in her throat as she walked up her garden path and unlocked the door to her little cottage, relieved to be home at last.

Without turning on the lights, Willow dropped her keys in the little basket by the door and made her way upstairs to bed.

****

She slept fitfully, her sleep disturbed by dreams she didn't remember upon waking, only aware of the tears dampening her cheeks and a feeling of unsettlement in her stomach. She had woken late in the afternoon, made herself a sandwich, and stared at the television without taking anything in for a couple of hours before crawling back into bed and falling asleep instantly.

Now it was morning again, and she was awake and couldn't get back to sleep. Heaving a frustrated sigh, she turned over onto her back to stare up at the ceiling.

Where was Ethan? Was he all right?

After everything that had happened, would he change his mind? Would he contact her? She didn't hold out much hope. She reached over to squint at her alarm clock. Nine thirty. May as well get up then.

Showered and changed, she sat hunched on the sofa, cradling a cup of coffee and staring at nothing. The hot coffee stung her lip where Mike's teeth had bitten into her, and she frowned, unwilling to reflect on Mike or Ethan. Glancing through the window, the cold, gray day matched her mood; the sky threatened more snow.

Good. Let it snow, let it cut the village off once again. She didn't want to go outside or see anyone ever again.

Willow caught herself, uneasy with the negative path her thoughts were taking, and set her mug down on the coffee table. No, that wasn't right. Hiding away in her cottage wasn't the answer. She refused to let Mike or Sam, or anyone, stop her from being herself.

Pushing herself up from the sofa, she took a white candle and her favorite amethyst crystal from her cabinet and placed them on the little carved wooden tray on the windowsill. Lighting the candle, she picked up the amethyst and enclosed it in her palm. She took a long, deep breath, closed her eyes, and quietly intoned a short incantation to drive away her fears. She repeated the incantation until she felt calmer and her fear had receded. A few minutes more of long, slow breaths filled her with a sense of determination, and she opened her eyes to stare through the window into the distance. She would not let them win. She was stronger than that.

Blowing out the candle, Willow returned the crystal to the cupboard and pulled on her coat, hat, scarf, and boots before she had the chance to change her mind.

Within minutes, she was striding down the pavement toward the village center, breathing in the sharp, cold air. It was nearly Christmas, her favorite time of year, and she was determined to be happy. Lost in thought and not really paying attention to her surroundings, she jumped when someone called her name. It was Gwen, standing in her doorway and waving at her.

"Willow!" Gwen beckoned to her. "I'm so pleased to see you. I was so worried. Please come in for a moment."

Her heart sank. Of course, everyone in the village would know what had happened by now and would no doubt want to know all the details. Rather reluctantly, she opened the gate and walked up to the front door.

"Come in, come in out of the cold."

She stepped into the warmth of Gwen's cottage and found herself pulled into a fierce, gardenia-scented hug. "Oh, Willow, I'm so pleased you're safe. I've heard all sorts of things."

Willow gave a weak smile. "I'll bet you have."

Gwen ushered her into the living room and bustled about making tea and coffee as Willow shrugged out of her coat and scarf. She took a deep breath, her eyes settling on the chair where Ethan had slept the night of the storm, the rug on which they had stood and shared their first kiss. She closed her eyes and sank on to the sofa, pushing thoughts of him away.

"You must tell me what happened," Gwen said after they were settled with a hot drink. "I've heard all sorts, such awful stories," she repeated. "Bob told me Ethan had been shot by a criminal on the run and that you shot the criminal. Depending upon whom you speak to, one or both of them are dead," she finished in a whisper, her eyes filling with tears. "Oh, Willow, please tell me it's not true."

"They're both alive. Ethan's okay," she said with a certainty she couldn't be sure of.

"Oh, I'm so relieved." Gwen put a hand to her chest. "But did you really shoot someone? Jonathan said it wasn't true. According to him, you were held hostage and Ethan was shot, but then you managed to free yourself and stabbed the criminal with a knife. You're the talk of the village."

At last Willow relaxed and laughed at the ridiculousness of it all. "Heavens, it's like Chinese whispers. Elements of truth in it all, but all of it quite wrong."

As Gwen continued to look at her expectantly, she sat back in her chair and took a sip of her coffee. "Okay, I'm going to tell you what happened, but then I'm not going to speak of it again. I can't face telling my story over and over again to everyone in the village, so if anyone asks, you're to tell them what really happened, okay?"

Gwen nodded, clearly happy with the responsibility for sharing her knowledge with the village.

"After the school fete, I was alone in the school." Willow hesitated, determined to be careful with how much she shared. "Someone involved in a case Ethan was working on knew he had been staying with me. He followed me to the school, and when I was alone he tried to kidnap me. I managed to hide until Ethan got there. Unfortunately, this man managed to trap Ethan and cut him fairly badly."

She paused and glanced across to Gwen, relieved to find a look of horror rather than eagerness for gossip in her friend's expression. Encouraged, she carried on. "I managed to sneak up on him and hit him with a rounders bat. Can you believe that? Ethan then knocked him unconscious, handcuffed him, and we called the police and an ambulance, and that was that. Not quite so exciting, really."

"Oh, Willow, you must have been so frightened," whispered Gwen. "But you were so brave. I can't imagine doing anything like that."

"I didn't feel brave at the time."

Gwen gave her an astute stare. "And now you just want to forget about it."

She nodded, staring into her coffee, trying not to cry.

"Quite right, too." There was a pause as they sat in companionable silence until Gwen spoke once more. "So just where were you going when I saw you striding past my window?"

Willow shrugged. "I don't really know. I just didn't want to let them…him win. I didn't want to be trapped in my house, frightened to go out." She gave a half smile. "So, I thought I would prove it. But I don't know where I was going. I was dreading bumping into anyone."

"You don't need to prove anything to anyone," said Gwen softly. "You've been through such an ordeal. It's perfectly normal if you want to hide away from the world for a little while. It doesn't mean you're weak or frightened. It means you just need time to heal.

"Go on home. Take care of yourself for once." Gwen frowned as a sudden thought came to her. "It's Christmas Eve. Is Ethan coming through later? You're not going to be spending the holiday on your own, are you? Because if you are, I can always tell Simon I'll stay here; I'm sure he won't mind." Gwen looked at her watch and bit her lip. "I'll need to let him know though because he'll be setting off soon to pick me up."

"There's absolutely no need. Yes, Ethan's coming to spend Christmas here with me," she lied with a bright smile. "Speaking of which, I'd better get back."

****

Willow locked her door, drew the curtains against the late afternoon sky and the wisps of snow gently drifting to the ground, and lit her favorite scented candle. Despite the relatively early hour, she felt she deserved the glass of Irish cream sitting on the coffee table and curled up on the sofa to watch a movie, any movie, just so long as it meant she didn't have to think.

The white lie she had told Gwen had been harder to repeat to her parents and Patrick when they had Skyped earlier, but she thought she had managed to pull it off. Her family had been in such good humor they had succeeded in lifting her mood, and she had decided not to tell them about Ethan, Mike, or Sam. That would be for another conversation, when it was less raw and she could look back on it with some distance.

It was warm and cozy in her little living room with the fire crackling against the glass of her log burner, and the tension eased across her shoulders as she began to relax.

The next moment, her peace was disturbed by a knock on her front door, and she shot to her feet, heart thumping in her chest. She stared at the door, an irrational fear preventing her from moving. Another knock sounded, making her jump once more.

Please let them go away.

"Willow?" The man's voice was muffled through the door. "Willow, it's Ethan."

She drew in a quick, painful breath and hurried to the door, but hesitated. What if it wasn't really him? What if it was a trick?

"Willow? Open the door. I know you're there."

She reached for the key and unlocked the door. Another hesitation, and then she pulled it open, gasping at the cold air rushing in from outside.

There he stood on her doorstep, blowing into his hands and stamping his feet against the cold. Ethan.

"Can I come in?"

"Yes, of course, I'm sorry." She stepped back immediately. "Please, come in."

She shut the door behind him as he shrugged painfully out of his jacket. He was pale, the sutured wound on his left temple surrounded by a bruise, a second bruise darkening his chin beneath the sore looking split lip. Her heart ached with longing as he turned to her, his expression one of concern.

"I'm sorry for turning up unannounced," he said quietly. "They kept me in overnight at the hospital, and I've only just finished at the station, but I was worried about you. I wanted to make sure you were okay."

She didn't respond, was struggling to hold it all together now he was here, and just stood there looking at him. His gaze was as sharp and intense as ever, and after a moment he held out his arms. "Come here."

Her face crumpled as the tears she had held in check all day finally spilled over, and she stepped into his embrace, huge sobs wracking her body as he wrapped his arms around her fiercely. She was finally home. Here in his embrace was home.

"It's okay, it's okay," he whispered over and over as he gently stroked her hair.

"I didn't think I was ever going to see you again," she sobbed against his chest. "They wouldn't tell me if you were okay. They just kept asking me questions and questions. They didn't believe me."

"I know. I'm sorry you had to go through that." Ethan pulled back to look at her. "I'm sorry for everything, Willow. It was all my fault, and I damn near got you killed. I should have listened to you."

She blinked, her breath hitching in her throat. “What…what do you mean?”

He pulled her to the sofa, and sat down, taking her hands in his. “When I saw you in the hall? Pointing that gun at Mike.” He swallowed and closed his eyes at the memory. “It was my worst nightmare, everything I’d been afraid of, drawing you into my world, putting you in danger and not being able to stop it.”

“I know. I’m sorry, Ethan—”

“But look at what you did. You saved my life… again.” He lifted her hands to his lips and kissed her knuckles. “And if you’re ever in that situation again…I want you to run. It was a bloody stupid thing you did… Stupid, but very brave.”

He brushed the hair from her face with his fingertips. “But you wouldn’t have been in that situation if I’d listened to you. How many times did I tell you, you were too trusting? And yet you didn’t trust Mike. You tried to tell me, and I didn’t listen. And because of that I almost got you killed.”

She reached up to smooth his forehead, smooth his worries away, her gaze taking in his battered face. “But you didn’t. You saved me, and I saved you. A team effort.”

He closed his eyes and swallowed. “When I looked up and saw you point the gun at Mike? In that moment, I knew that if we got out of this alive, I couldn’t walk away from you anymore.”

He hesitated for a moment, his gaze searching her face. “I knew I’d fallen in love with you.”

She caught her breath and simply stared at him, hardly able to hear anything over the thudding of her heart beating in her chest.

Ethan smiled. “It’s Christmas Eve, and for the first time in forever I’m not going to be working. And I know after everything that’s happened it might not be what you want, but what do you say to spending Christmas with me?”

She blinked for a moment in surprise, relief suddenly flowing through her body, and allowed herself to smile. “I thought you didn’t like Christmas, that it wasn’t your thing?”

“I’ve had a recent change of heart…about a few things.” He leaned forward and kissed her carefully, trying not to aggravate his injured lip. “So, what do you say?”

“You’re not too worried about getting stuck in Brigadoon?” Willow smiled against his lips, felt his answering smile.

“It’s a risk I’m willing to take.”

A word about the author…

I love to write heartwarming, contemporary romance and romantic suspense novels, with characters I really want my readers to engage with. I live in the beautiful East Riding of Yorkshire in the UK and, although I work full-time in the public sector, my favorite pastime, when not writing, is wandering around old stately homes and dreaming of a fairytale life.

I enjoy engaging with both readers and other authors and am a proud member of the Romantic Novelist Association.

https://elliegrayauthor.wordpress.com

Thank you for purchasing
this publication of The Wild Rose Press, Inc.

For questions or more information
contact us at
info@thewildrosepress.com.

The Wild Rose Press, Inc.
www.thewildrosepress.com

CPSIA information can be obtained
at www.ICGtesting.com
Printed in the USA
LVHW081752271021
701715LV00013B/366

9 781509 236336